Granny was a Buffer Girl

'I hate the stuff,' Granny Dorothy said. 'Money. It rots you. We've never had much of it, and I'm glad. I wanted to be rich once upon a time. Not now.'

'You hadn't much chance, marrying me,' Albert laughed.

'It's not money that matters, anyway. It's your health,' said Katie. That was because she was an outsider, and didn't know how we do things in our house and what all this chatter was about. But even before her words sank us into silence my dad had brought in the bottle of special wine, and had filled up all our glasses again and stood with his own raised. 'Don't forget the Birthday Celebration,' he said, smiling with the mood of the party talk, his traitor voice low and thick. 'Let's drink to Danny.'

And we all stood up and were silent.

It's hard for Jess to imagine what it will be like, separated from her family and friends and the place she has always known. And before she goes, Jess wants to share all the family secrets – its love stories and its ghost stories too . . .

D1538425

Berlie Doherty

Granny was a Buffer Girl

COLLINS

LIONS · TRACKS

For Dad, Mike,
Gloria, Paul and Mattie.

With thanks to Dave Sheasby,
who asked me to write
Granny was a Buffer Girl
for BBC Radio Sheffield,
and to Jackie Ruff,
who talked to me about buffer girls.

First published in Great Britain
by Methuen Children's Books Ltd
First published in Lions Tracks 1988
Third impression May 1989

Lions Tracks is an imprint of
the Children's Division, part of
the Collins Publishing Group,
8 Grafton Street, London W1X 3LA

Printed and bound in Great Britain by
William Collins Sons & Co. Ltd, Glasgow

Contents

1 Celebrations

'Hurry up, Grandpa!' I shouted. 'We're celebrating tonight.' Grandpa waved. He hadn't heard what I'd said. He was playing bowls with the old people. He'd known some of them nearly all his life. He nursed his bowl as he waited to roll it, then he stepped forward on to the black disc, hitching his trouser leg as he bent his knee and showing an incongruous flash of red sock. When he'd released his bowl he stood with his feet turned in and his veined hands dangling free, as a child might, watching as it whispered over the soft turf and smiling when it clocked against the jack.

I moved away from the green, hurt suddenly to see how old he was. The sky was rushing to early sunset. The clouds were tinged with apricot. I could see our house from here, and the spread of Sheffield away from it, with street lights already pricking out the way the roads went. I was on the top of the Bole Hills, the windiest green in the world, Grandpa told me. There was a quarry here once. Some people say it's really 'bone hills' because it was built on an old tip, and when I think I'm standing on the bottles and bones and crumbling waste of long-dead families I feel dizzy, as if this tiny moment of the present and all the moments of my future are slipping away fast from me. But Grandpa tells me it's 'bowl hills', because there's a bowling green on the top, and that seems much kinder to me.

'Time to go then, Jess, is it?' Grandpa came up behind me, the bowls knocking together in the little bag Mum gave him for Christmas.

He's smaller than me.

'Are you coming down for tea, Little Man?' I asked him.

'I won't say no, if it's worth eating. You haven't cooked it, have you?'

'Not this time, Grandpa.'

'That's all right then. I'll risk it.'

He grunted as the path steepened down, and I waited for him. He wouldn't want me to help him.

'Was it a good game?'

'Grand. I'm better than any of that lot now, I reckon. Bridie should have been there. She always says I don't send them right, but I do. She'd be surprised. I've just played the best game of my life.'

He always talks about my nan as though she's just slipped out to the shops for a bit, and will be back home soon. Perhaps he's forgotten that she died a year ago.

'If you're winning at bowls today you'll be able to celebrate, Little Man,' I said. 'Along with the rest of us.'

'Why, what are you celebrating? Not getting married, are you?'

I'd just said goodbye to Steve. Just.

'Not yet, Grandpa. I'm not that daft.'

'What's happening, then?' He stopped, taking deep, slow breaths. I shouldn't walk so fast when I'm with him.

'Well, for a start, I'm off to France tomorrow for my year abroad.'

'How come?'

'It's part of my University course. You know that. I'm always telling you.'

'Well, this is a real celebration, then. We're getting rid of you at last.' And then he fumbled round in his pockets for a handkerchief and blew into it noisily. 'I'm sorry J-Jess. I didn't mean to say that.'

'I know that, Little Man. We're always saying things we don't mean.'

Perhaps it was something to do with the manner of my nan's going. She hadn't been ill. She just didn't wake up

8

one morning. Everyone said it was the best way to go, but I couldn't believe that. Surely she'd have wanted a minute or two to remember her seventy years, and to say goodbye? And my mother had said a strange thing as we were walking away in the sunshine from the Catholic cemetery at Rivelin. She'd said, 'Now we've another life to celebrate.' *Life*! So we'd had the celebrations at our house, and afterwards Dad had sent up all his pigeons for her, and Grandpa Jack had stood with his cap in his hand, watching them and watching them, till they'd all fluttered down and clustered back into their loft.

His house is so quiet now.

By the time we reached home Mum had already drawn the curtains. The garden smelt of bonfires, and Dad's wellingtons propped each other up by the step. My brother John came to the door as we opened it and took Grandpa's bag and cap to put with the coats, and John's girlfriend Katie gave Grandpa a hug as if she was one of the family already. She was my best friend at school.

'Where's Steve?' she asked, surprised. He's her brother.

'I didn't invite him to tea,' I said. I looked past her at John. I hadn't wanted Katie to be here, either. Perhaps John and Katie were closer than I thought. Perhaps they would stay together.

'Is he coming on later, then?' Katie asked. We went everywhere as a four usually.

I shook my head, doubt making me unhappy again. 'I've already said goodbye to him,' I said.

Little Grandpa Jack had made his way into the front room to join my other grandparents. Granny Dorothy was coughing over a glass of sherry. She'd had her hair newly permed and dyed for tonight, and was wearing the bluebell-coloured dress that she always keeps for these occasions. Grandad Albert pulled the ring of a can of beer back so it was foaming ready for Grandpa Jack as soon as he found his chair. I went to set the table. I could hear Mum and Dad in the kitchen, arguing about the gravy. I was already feeling nervous.

'Ready!' Mum shouted.

John and Katie brought the old folks in and settled them in their chairs while Mum and Dad served out. There was wine – Dad's home brew from a kit. It always gives me hiccups. It always makes me sad.

'Here's to Jess!' Dad said. 'Off to see the world!'

Mum squeezed my hand.

'I left home when I was your age, Jess,' Dad went on. 'Your grandad said it would make a man of me.'

Grandad Albert laughed. 'What did Dorothy used to say? You'd end up a dirty old man with no stamps on your National Insurance card . . . .'

'I don't suppose Jess is too happy about going away now,' Granny Dorothy said. 'Not if she's leaving her young man behind.'

'Grandpa Jack's got something to celebrate,' I said quickly. 'He played his best game of bowls today.'

'I did,' he said. 'I think it's because I've had my hair cut. I can balance better now.'

'There's nothing there to cut, Jack,' Grandad Albert said. 'It'd be easier to pluck it out!' His own hair is thick and white, and he's a big man, like my dad, like John is becoming. 'If we're boasting today, them's my chrysanths on the sideboard. Look at them. Big as your fist.' His flowers are the colour of marmalade, heavy and sullen. 'Like lions,' he said. 'Beautiful.'

'Granny . . . .'

She was coughing again, wheezing and spitting into her handkerchief. It took her a long time to get over this bout but she came up smiling. 'I shouldn't drink wine,' she said. 'It goes straight to my windpipe.'

'What are you celebrating, Granny?'

'Celebrating?' she held her glass out for Dad to fill again.

Mum frowned at him. 'Well, getting our Louie into a home, I suppose, if you can call that something to celebrate. I know she'll be better off there, but I still feel it's a terrible thing to do to her. I do, Albert, it's no good arguing. I've only got one sister now, and I feel as if I've let her down. That awful marriage she had. She's only had five years to enjoy herself. Go on, Michael. Fill my glass. Fill it up.'

Dad pulled a face at my mum and did as he was told. 'Anyone want to know what I did today?' he said. 'I ran as far as Rivelin Dams. That's the furthest I've ever done. I think I'll go in for the Sheffield Marathon next June.'

'I think we'll join you, Dad,' said John. 'What d'you think, Katie?'

The look she shared with him excluded all of us. 'Better than sitting down doing nothing all day.'

'It gets you, running does,' Dad warned them. 'It's like a fever, or a drug.'

'I might have a go myself,' said little Grandpa Jack. 'I've heard of chaps older than me doing marathons.'

I cleared away the dirty plates and stood in the kitchen listening to their chatter and laughter. Dread lay in the hollow of my stomach. I wished they'd get this bit over with and get on with the important thing. This was their ritual, a gentle nursing back towards the old, bad memory. I could hear Katie's laughter among the rest. John must love her, then, to have brought her tonight. I wasn't ready to share it with Steve yet. Maybe that was how you could tell whether you really loved someone or not. I'd said goodbye to Steve at the bottom of the Bole Hills, just before I'd set off to fetch Grandpa down. He'd been on his bike, bending down to me because he was so much taller than me and because the wind was playing havoc with our voices.

'Can I come to the station to see you off tomorrow?' he'd said.

'No. I'd rather you didn't.'

'You're glad you're going, aren't you?'

'Course I am. I'm excited.'

'You know what I mean. Away from me. You're glad.'

'I'll be home for Christmas,' I reminded him, helpless. I don't know why I hadn't been able to say goodbye to him. It was nothing to do with wanting to hurt him.

'You'll find someone else by then,' he said quietly, not looking at me, and then he drove his pedals down and rode off, head down into the wind.

'I'll write, Steve. I'll see you soon,' I shouted.

I was a snake, shedding its skin; a glistening, fleshy thing; a jewel in dark grass. I shuddered, thrilled, scared.

'I don't know if you'd call mine a celebration or not,' Mum was saying as I took the tray of ice-creams in. 'I've been offered a full term's supply teaching. If it's anything like the last school I'd rather not have it.'

'Money's good though, on supply,' Dad said, and his look said 'You should be glad of any job these days.'

'But that's all it's worth, at a school like that. The money. There should be more to it than that, especially with a job like teaching.'

'Like growing flowers,' said Grandad Albert. 'I know, Josie. There's some jobs you can't put a price on, not when you love doing them. Money's a bonus.'

'I hate the stuff,' Granny Dorothy said. 'Money. It rots you. We've never had much of it, and I'm glad. I wanted to be rich once upon a time. Not now.'

'You hadn't much chance, marrying me,' Albert laughed.

'It's not money that matters, anyway. It's your health,' said Katie. That was because she was an outsider, and didn't know how we do things in our house, and what all

12

this chatter was about. But even before her words sank us into silence my dad had brought in the bottle of special wine, and had filled up all our glasses again and stood with his own raised. 'Don't let's forget the Birthday Celebration,' he said, smiling with the mood of the party talk, his traitor voice low and thick. 'Let's drink to Danny.'

And we all stood up, and were silent.

After the meal I went into the downstairs room we still call Danny's. My record player is in there, and John's dartboard, but we don't go in there much. Mum wants the room to be used more. She keeps her typewriter in there, but she carries it into the living-room to use it.

There's a photograph of Danny on the wall. Just his face. He's got his head back, laughing. He's about ten there. I only ever see that photograph face. When I try to think of him as he was last time I saw him, that laughing face slides in front, getting in the way.

I put a record on. It's a special song that reminds me of someone I met at a disco once. I sat on the bed that used to be Danny's and sang the words softly to myself. I could see our cat, Paddy, on his twilight prowl around the apple tree. The fruits gleamed silver, heavy among the silver-green leaves and the dark branches.

Mum looked in on her way down from the bathroom and put the light on. 'OK, love?' she asked.

'Of course I am. Why shouldn't I be?'

She came in and drew the curtains. 'Thinking about Danny?'

'Isn't that what today's all about?'

'That, and other things. D'you know what I've just been thinking? I'm going to have two empty rooms in the house now. Perhaps that's a metaphor for middle age, Jess. Empty rooms.'

The record clicked as it finished. We sat in the silence.

I wanted to tell Mum something that I'd never been able

to say to her before. If I left it till I came back home I might never be able to say it. I might be a different person.

'I want to say something about Danny.'

She waited, sad.

'I said a terrible thing to him, that day.'

'I know,' she said.

'Would he have heard me, Mum?'

She shook her head. 'It was already too late.' She pressed her eyes with the tips of her fingers, the way she sometimes does when she takes off her reading glasses; tired. 'I'll tell you a secret, shall I? I said a terrible thing once. I was in the park near the children's hospital, by that little pond. Your father and I were watching Danny throwing bread to the ducks. I knew what was going to happen to him then. I was trying to protect him from his own future, I suppose, and I was trying to protect myself, and I said a terrible thing. We mustn't be ashamed of what we say at times like that. It's about love.'

'Katie's going, everyone,' John called from the kitchen.

'Mum, what *did* you say?' I asked. She patted my hand and stood up to see her guest out.

'Bye everyone,' Katie shouted. 'Jess! You're going tomorrow!' She came in to hug me.

'Give my love to Steve,' I said.

Mum went in to talk to the grandparents while Dad and I cleared away the rest of the dishes. I couldn't catch Mum's eye. At last John came back from seeing Katie home. He'd run from her house and came in panting. You could feel the heat steaming off him. He flopped into a chair.

'You ran to Rivelin Dams, Dad?' he said, gasping. 'I don't believe it!'

Dad grinned, proud.

'I wish B-Bridie was here,' said Grandpa Jack. 'How she loves a party. They used to have singing and dancing and story-telling all through the night at her house.'

'Dad,' my Mum said. 'Tell us about you and Bridie.'

'That'd be giving secrets away, Josie,' he said. But he looked wistful, as if he was longing for the story-telling days of his youth.

'You tell your secrets, and I'll tell mine,' said Granny Dorothy. 'I'll tell you something that Albert doesn't know, even. My best secret.'

Mum did catch my eye then, and her look promised me that I wouldn't be going away from home without sharing all its secrets, all its love stories, and all its ghost stories too.

2 Bridie and Jack

As soon as the sharp sound of her father's feet had died away, Bridie Rooney slipped on her coat and hat, called goodbye, and stepped out into the yard. There in the darkness she powdered her face, discreetly, away from her mother's disapproval. She could hear her sisters giggling in the doorway behind her.

'Will you get in!' she said sharply. 'There's nothing to laugh at out here!'

They scurried back into the kitchen. Bridie waited a moment for the sound of her mother coming, dabbed her powder-puff along her nose, and snapped her compact shut.

She ran down the street to the main road, glancing round to make sure there was no sign of her father, and then across to the tram stop. As she stepped on to the tram she was aware of curious eyes on her and she blushed self-consciously. She was used to being looked at: something of a beauty – even her mother acknowledged that. She had strong Irish features and thick, dark hair and blue eyes; she drew many covetous glances, whether she sought them or not. She dressed well too; all the money that was left over from paying her mother for her keep went on clothes, and tonight she was wearing a new winter coat that hung like a cape from her shoulders, and a little blue helmet hat with a parrot embroidered on the side. You'd think she was one of the rich girls, instead of being a cobbler's daughter. They were proud of her, her parents, though they would never have admitted it even to the parish priest in the confessional.

She nodded and smiled her way down the tram, embarrassed by the glances cast at her, wishing she'd worn her plain grey hat. When the conductor came for her fare she smiled at him modestly.

'Who's this?' he asked loudly. 'Old King Cole?'

There was a shout of laughter from the passengers and Bridie turned away, uncomfortable, trying to catch her reflection in the window of the tram. She opened her bag, felt around for her little mother-of-pearl hand mirror, and slid it on to her knee. A flame of disbelief burned across her neck. She picked up the mirror to catch full view of her face – her cheeks, with two black rings; her nose, and her chin as black as a seaside minstrel's!

She fumbled wildly in her bag again for a handkerchief and as she did so the lid of her powder-box lifted and the contents spilled out on to her hands. Soot! Her mind flashed back to tea-time, when her sisters had been scraping the fire-back and giggling helplessly. She held up the mirror again, watching the slow tears trickle through the rings of soot on her cheeks. The tram lurched to a halt and she clutched her bag, held on to her hat and clattered down the planks. She jumped off, ran blindly down the street, and swung at last into the brightness of Victoria Station, straight into the arms of a young man.

'Hello!' he said, steadying her. 'It's a chimney sweep!'

Tears of anger coursed down her cheeks.

'Leave me alone,' she sobbed. 'I want the Ladies' Room.'

When she came out again, her cheeks red and shining from the scrubbing she'd given them, and her hair hanging damply to her shoulders, the young man was waiting for her. He folded up his paper and walked across to her as she stood blinking in the station bustle.

'That's better,' he said. 'I come here for my annual wash, too.'

She waited, mortified.

'I'm not laughing at you,' he went on. 'I was worried about you. That's wh-why I've w-waited.'

It was his stammer that disarmed her. When he offered her a coffee and a slice of cream cake at the Corner House she gratefully accepted, without a second thought for the young man she was supposed to be meeting, who wasn't so good-looking, and who must by now have hopelessly abandoned his vigil for her. With a guilty look round for her spying sisters she accompanied him to the coffee-shop. She watched him appreciatively as he talked. He was a bright young blade, with dark hair and moustache and brown lively eyes, and a stutter that every so often broke across his animated speech and belied his air of confidence charmingly. He wore a neat suit, and spats, and carried yellow kid gloves and a silver-topped cane. His style matched her own. But it didn't take them long to discover that they had little else in common.

Bridie came from a large brood of Irish Catholics. 'Hundreds of us' she told him, squashed up together somehow in the tiny rooms of a terraced house in Solly Street. Her father kept a strict and vigorous watch on all his daughters. 'If any of youse girls gets yerselves in trouble with the fellers,' he would shout at any sign of coy immodesty, 'I'll break every bone in your body, so help me.' Bridie knew he meant it. He and his wife paraded the girls across the road to church every Sunday and holy day, proud of their beauty and hostile to any unseemly glances. And it went without saying that they never even took the non-Catholic glances into consideration. They would marry the girls off to good Catholic boys of the parish, when the time came.

Jack was the son of a headmaster. He lived along with his elderly parents in a fine, quiet house – his father always maintained there the dignity that his office as headmaster required. He kept secret the fact that his only surviving child was a great disappointment, as he was only of average intelligence and showed little interest in anything except his clothes and his motor-bike. Jack's father consoled himself with his books and his music, leaving his wife to see to the boy; and she, thoughtful and sad since the loss of her first two boys in the Great War, anxiously watched him grow up. 'So long as he's happy,' she always said to her husband, 'we must be thankful.' They were a deeply religious couple. And if there was one thing they disliked, it was a Catholic.

Jack walked Bridie back to her tram-stop, knowing that he'd have to see her again. He pressed her hand warmly as her tram drew up.

'I w-want to see you tomorrow,' he blurted out.

'Where?' The tram had stopped.

'Here?'

'It'd have to be straight from work.' She was climbing on.

He wanted to ask what time that would be but couldn't get the words out. Never mind, he thought, I'll wait for her all night if I have to. She waved goodbye to him as the tram moaned off, but as it swayed through the dark streets she realised that it was already way past her bed-time and that her father would be home. She hurried away from her tram-stop, rounded her street, saw a triangle of light thrown across the cobbles, and knew that he was on the doorstep, waiting for her.

'What time d'you call this, you little hussy?' His voice echoed round the houses.

'Half past nine, Dad.' She knew it was no use lying. Lying was just as much of a sin as disobedience was.

'Get in that house and up them stairs to your bed!'

She dodged under his arm and ran across the room where her brother Will was preparing his bath in front of the fire, and her mother sat darning at the table.

'Up them stairs!' roared her father as Bridie stopped at the dresser to break off a hunk of bread. 'And say your Act of Contrition.' She scampered away from him up to her room, flung off her clothes in the darkness and jumped into bed.

Her father sat down at the table with his head in his hands. 'Never have daughters, Will,' he said. 'What d'you suppose she's been up to, till this time of night?'

'Shinanikin'' said Will, gloating, from his bath. He was the only son.

'Aye, shinanikin', I've no doubt. They're more worry than they're worth, girls are. What are we doing with so many daughters, Nancy, and all this worry they bring us?'

'What's this nonsense?' his wife said calmly. 'Who'd be keeping your house clean for you, with me helping you with the boots, if it wasn't for the girls? Who'd cook your meals?'

There was no answer to that.

Upstairs Bridie's sisters pretended to be asleep and squinted at her in the darkness, waiting for her abuse and their punishment. They hardly dared breathe.

But Bridie had forgotten all about their trick with the soot. She snuggled down into her warm bedclothes, smiling at the thought of the dapper young man at Victoria Station, and was cosily snoring long before the sisters lying wide-eyed with suspense beside her.

From then on Bridie and Jack spent every spare minute together, but secretly. Jack dared himself to come as far as the end of her street for her, but no further. He had a motor-bike, a huge eight horse power Matchless; she grew used to the sound of it and would be there waiting for him long before he roared into view. When spring came he took her into Derbyshire on it, and was proud of the stir caused by his throaty engine and his striking passenger. Once they got hopelessly lost, frantically weaving in and out of country lanes with only the cows to watch them as the sky blackened and the stars burst through like flowers. At last they came across a procession of miners, trudging their way to work.

'Where are we?' shouted Jack, while beneath them the huge machine snorted and shook like a bull waiting to charge.

'Maltby,' said one of them, winking at Bridie as he went past.

'Maltby! Can you find you way back now?' Bridie shouted.

'If we've got enough petrol I can,' said Jack.

'I don't want to go back, anyway,' moaned Bridie. 'I'd rather be dead than in our house when my dad finds out.'

Grimly Jack rode her home. She slipped off the bike right at the top of the street and without even saying goodbye to him ran like the wind to her house, as if saving a minute over these last few yards was going to save her from the beating she knew would be coming. Amazingly, though, her dad had come home that night too tight with drink to ask about the girls, and had found his bed and stayed there. Bridie's mother was awake though. She heard the bike in the distance, listened out for running feet, crept downstairs, and pulled open the door just as Bridie reached it. She slapped the girl's face so hard that her own hand smarted the rest of the night.

'If you've done a sin I'll turn you out of house and home!' she hissed, slapping her again with her other hand.

'I haven't. Honest to God I haven't.'

'And it's Sunday by now, d'you know that! I'll be watching you when you go up for Holy Communion, my girl. I'll be watching you!'

Just before they had reached Bridie's end of town Jack had shouted to her, 'I'll come up tomorrow and explain everything to your parents.'

'No, don't,' she'd begged. But by the time Sunday Mass was over and done with and her father had gone out for his Sunday pleasures she was half-hoping he would come, after all. She wanted her mother to know him. She told her sisters that he might come and they waited upstairs, tense with excitement. Bridie, white-faced, stayed in the back room. She didn't want him to come. It was too late. Her father would be home soon. Why didn't he come now? When at last the throb of his engine was heard outside she shuddered in horror. There was a shriek from upstairs: 'It's him! It's our Bridie's young man!' And she sat in the dark room, unable to move, while Jack knocked on the door and the girls clattered gaily downstairs. But it was her brother, Will, who opened the door to him and stood learning on the door-jamb, eyeing Jack laconically.

'Did you want something?' His blue eyes were full of humour, watching the young man's nervousness. Jack looked past him at the five laughing girls. No sign of Bridie. Where was the girl? Out?

His dreaded stammer returned.

'Is your B-B-Bridie in?'

'Wh-huh-hu-what if she is?'

'Sh-she's expecting me.'

'She's expecting C-C-C-Christmas an' all.'

'Who is it, our Will?' came a woman's voice, curious, from inside. Just then Bridie came from the back room. She was cold with nervousness.

'Hello, Jack,' she said quietly. 'Won't you come in a minute?'

Will winked at his sisters, who flattened themselves against the wall to let Jack pass. He was wearing a sporting jacket with breeches and long woollen stockings, and the plump little woman busy at the stove stared at him in amazement.

'What's this creature?'

'This is Mr Hall, Mum, a friend of mine.' Bridie spoke slowly and coldly. 'He's come to explain why I was so late last night.'

'Like the blazes he has!'

But Jack and his charm triumphed. He told her that he could see why she had six beautiful daughters, and how much pleasure it had given him to show Bridie the Derbyshire that he had always loved, and how he would take her, Mrs Rooney, she'd only to ask, he'd make sure she didn't fall off; and all the while Bridie was darting anxious glances at the clock on the mantelpiece and little Ann was hopping inside and out to keep a watchout for her father.

'Would you like to have a look at it, Mrs Rooney?' asked Jack. 'You'll see, it's as safe as houses.'

'I would!' she said, excited. She gave the potatoes a prod and slid them back into the fire-oven, and the whole family followed Jack out into the road.

The machine, like a beast at rest, lay waiting. Jack, confident, strode up to it while the girls crowded round him and curtains on either side of the Rooney's twitched. He glanced up and down the flat street – not a good place to start. He ran the bike down to the end, with Annie and Peg running after; and back, red-faced, panting, and as he passed the house for the third time the thing coughed and sputtered and burst into life. The crowd cheered.

'Come on, B–B–Bridie!' he called.

He flung himself across his bike, his belly over the saddle, and heaved himself into a sitting position, while the Matchless roared and shivered beneath him. Bridie ran after him, jammed her hat down firmly on her head, hoisted up her skirt and swung herself over the back of the machine. They came in a huge circle past the house with a roar of triumph, everyone shouting and waving, dust swirling round them and small stones flying, curved again in a magnificent swoop – lost control, and careered in hiccups of screaming zig-zags towards the house, missed it, and came to rest, juddering and gasping, on the front step of next-door-but-one.

'If that's you, Bridie Rooney, I'll break every bone in

your body!'

Bridie and Jack struggled to get free, arms and legs flailing, shaking splinters of black front door off their clothing. They backed away from the angry figure bearing down on them from the end of the street.

'It's my dad!' Bridie could hardly speak.

Jack grabbed his hat in one hand and Bridie in the other and they charged off in the other direction, with Bridie's father shouting and panting after them and Peg and Annie and some dogs after him, and in the doorway stood Bridie's mother, dabbing her eyes with the corner of her pinny and not knowing whether it was tears of laughter or of grief that she was wiping away.

They sat, bumping together on the back seat of the tram, chasing each other's thoughts all the way to the terminus.

'You know what I want, don't you, Bridie?' Jack said. It was hopeless, and he knew it, but the thing had to be said. 'I want to m-marry you.'

She didn't look at him. 'Will you turn?'

'I couldn't be a Catholic. You know I couldn't.'

'Then my father will never let us get married.'

The tram trundled them slowly down to the city. If Jack married her he would never be forgiven, he knew that. It would be like an act of treachery to his parents. And his mother had lost two sons already. He loved her far too much to hurt her.

'They've always told me how wicked non-Catholics are,' Bridie whispered. 'And here am I, in love with one. What am I doing, in love with a Protestant?'

'It just happened,' Jack consoled her. 'You couldn't help it.'

Bridie felt her cheeks burning as she slipped her hand into his. It was not to be stopped, this love. Yet there was a deep sadness between them like the weight of years. They sat in the tram watching the blue sparks flash, and still they said nothing. The tram brought them back to the stop near Bridie's street. They got off together.

'There's no answer,' said Jack. 'There's nothing we can do.'

'Unless we get married anyway,' said Bridie, daring.

'And don't tell them, you mean?'

'Tell them after. They couldn't do anything about it then. It's our lives. I don't mind marrying a Protestant.'

'I don't mind marrying a Catholic,' said Jack, surprised.

They went slowly back to her street, still too deeply troubled to say more. She went in to her own house and helped her mother to serve out the Sunday dinner, and her father held back his anger for once, watching her strange sadness. Jack left some money with the people whose front door he'd damaged and wheeled his bike away.

And a month later they were married. It was in the middle of a working day for both of them. They had a meal out at the Corner House at the end of the day and then Jack went to his house and Bridie went to hers. The room they were to rent fully furnished wasn't to be ready till the following week. They decided that they would leave the telling of the news till the last minute, when their room would be ready for them to escape to, and no one would be able to do anything about it. Bridie lay awake all night between her sisters, watching the soft movement of the curtains at the open windows; afraid.

Next day was Sunday, when she was to go to Mass with her family. She sat with her sister Polly. It was cool and dark in the church. Sunlight thrust through the coloured panes of the stained glass windows, jewelling the benches and the backs of the bent figures at prayer. The altar was bright with June flowers, and the air sweet with the scent of them, and of the incense burning. She loved this church. The priest's murmured chant reminded her of the drone of insects busy in summer gardens. The rich and quiet ceremony of the Mass was as familiar to her as family rituals; it was part of her life. The congregation sat back for the sermon, and the priest, who had christened her and all her young relations, sought out her eyes and spoke only to her.

'Deny your God, who loves you,' he told her, 'and you will spend Eternity in the Everlasting Flames of Hell.' His words burned into every pore of her flesh. 'And one moment of Hell is the span of your entire lifetime,' he reminded her, just her, his voice like a spider in the crack of her ear, creeping down through all the mysterious veins and cells and sinews of her body to enter the pale cloudy substance somewhere underneath her bones which was where she felt her soul to be. 'And every moment that is as long as a lifetime is as tiny as one grain of sand dropped among all the grains of sand on the shores of infinity, and there will be no counting of them, for these shores are without end ... without end ....' There was a coughing and shuffling of feet as he left the pulpit. Her mother and sisters stood up around her for the singing of the creed and Bridie leaned forward, letting the sweet quavering voices drench her. She felt Polly kneeling down to her. 'Bridie ... Bridie ....'

'Polly,' she whispered back. 'I married Jack yesterday.'

'That's wonderful,' said Polly. 'Won't you stand up, Bridie, and sing! That's wonderful.'

After Mass, when Mr Rooney had gone for his drink, Polly made Bridie tell her mother. After all, Mrs Rooney wasn't all that surprised. She knew love when she saw it. She was disappointed, though.

'I love weddings,' she said. 'I've been planning yours for years, and here am I, not even invited.'

'Perhaps we'll have another wedding, in the church,' said Bridie wistfully. She would have the choir, and her little sisters all in pale dresses, and the blessing of the priest ....

'Well, that would be better than nothing,' said Mrs Rooney. 'Could you not have found a good Catholic boy in the first place though, from the parish, and saved all this messing?'

'Mother! You've seen what they're like.'

Her mother nodded. There hadn't been much choice in her day, either. 'We've never had a convert in the family before,' she sighed. 'But I suppose it'll just have to do.'

'Mother, you don't understand!' gasped Bridie. 'Jack can't turn Catholic.'

'What's this? Can't?' Mrs Rooney closed her eyes against this terrible news.

'Won't, then,' said Bridie. She'd rather face the priest in the confessional than break this to her mother. 'Jack will never be a Catholic, Mother. It'd be lying to himself if he did.'

'Somebody's got to lie,' Mrs Rooney moaned. 'Who's going to tell your father this news? I'm not.'

'I can't tell lies, Mother. It's a sin.' Bridie was cold to the bone.

'So's your marriage a sin, Bridie Rooney. Don't you know that? In the eyes of the Church you're not married at all. And there's no marrying that Protestant at the Sacred Heart. Ever. And where is the man, anyway? What kind of a "husband" is he, leaving you to sort this mess out all by yourself? What kind of a marriage d'you call this, for goodness sake?'

Jack was at home, brooding. He didn't know how to begin to tell his mother that he'd married a Catholic. Yet he couldn't bring himself to see Bridie again until he had told his mother, until he'd made it all right with her. Then he toyed with the idea of waiting till the time came for him to take his furnished room and just telling his mother he was moving in with a pal from work. Even that would hurt her. He sat by the fireside two nights after his wedding, prodding and prodding the coals to make them spurt, knowing nothing of what he was doing but aware that his mother's sad eyes were fixed on him, and that he couldn't meet them.

'What's up with you, Jack?' she said to him at last.

'Nothing, Ma. L-leave me alone.' He cracked a coal open, so the flames burst through. Shadows flung frenzied arms across the walls and ceiling; his eyes were set deep into his face, in pockets of darkness. He'd never kept anything from her before. 'It would break her heart if I told her,' he thought to himself, while she watched him. 'But what am I doing, sitting here night after night, when I've a young wife waiting for me?'

He flung the poker down and ran out. It rolled backwards and forwards on the hearth, backwards and forwards, till at last Jack's mother picked it up and stood it in its holder and went over to the window. She watched him, sorrowing for him, as he revved his motor-bike up in the yard.

'Where's the boy gone at this time of night?' her husband called, annoyed, from his study.

'He's not a boy,' she said. 'He's a grown man, Joseph. And he's sick with worry.'

Bridie was in bed when Jack arrived. He didn't know whether she slept in the front or the back of the house, so had no way of warning her. He banged on the door and Mr Rooney opened it to him.

'What's up?' he asked, not knowing Jack.

'I've c-come for B-B-Bridie.'

'What d'you mean, you've come for bloody Bridie?' The whole house was awake with the man's shouting.

Jack saw her on the stairs, and she gave him strength.

'She's my wife.'

He couldn't help smiling, in spite of his terror. Nor could she.

Mr Rooney turned round and pulled Bridie down to the door.

'Is this true?'

'Yes, Father,' she whispered. 'We were married Saturday.'

Mr Rooney stared at her, doubt and astonishment and rage chasing each other across his face. A surge of nostalgia swelled up in him. Nothing was dearer to him than romance.

'How old are you, Bridie?' he asked his daughter.

'Twenty-one.'

'You're a child yet, for all that,' he said softly. 'You must take care of her, young man.'

He pushed Bridie out on to the doorstep and shut the door before the moisture in his eyes betrayed him.

'But, Father,' said Bridie, hammering on the door. 'I'm still in my nightie.'

'You've made your bed, my girl,' he said roughly, pushing to the bolts on the other side. 'Now you must lie on it.'

'Now what do we do?' asked Bridie.

'We go and tell my parents,' said Jack. 'Together. We should have done it in the first place. We've done it all wrong.'

He took off his jacket and put it round her shoulders, and after a bit of revving and kicking and running up and down the street he got the Matchless started and they set off on the long ride to his parents' house. Bridie snuggled against his back and closed her eyes. He grinned.

'Happy?' he shouted.

She nodded and smiled cosily, even though she knew he couldn't see her doing it. He started singing, with the wind gasping into his breath and his voice jerking with every rut and stone on the road. 'I'd like to take you, on a slow boat to China . . . .' And Bridie started laughing, shouting with laughing, and they knew that nothing as terrible and as wonderful as this would ever happen to them again.

Jack's mother heard them coming. 'Joseph,' she called. 'He's back.' She opened the door to them and she and her husband stood in the polished hallway in silence as Bridie and Jack came in, hand in hand, their singing and their laughter quite gone.

'This is Bridie,' Jack said, looking at his father. 'She's a Catholic, and she's my wife.'

Bridie had oil on her nightie. Her hands and her cheeks were red with the wind and her hair was in a terrible state. Jack's father went back into the drawing-room, where they heard him putting his books back on their shelves.

'You can't stay here,' said Jack's mother to Bridie. 'I'm sorry.'

The three stood, saying nothing. Never before had Jack been so aware of the hall clock's loud tick.

'I've nothing else to wear,' said Bridie.

'Of course. Come up to my room and I'll find you something.'

Neither of the women looked at each other. Bridie followed Jack's mother up the polished stairs.

'We've nowhere to go,' said Jack when his mother came down again. 'We've a furnished room, but it's not ours till Saturday.'

'*You* have a good home here,' she reminded him. She joined her husband in the drawing-room.

More sad than angry, Jack went upstairs and stuffed some clothes into his small knapsack. He'd no idea what they would do. He came out of his room again when he heard Bridie going downstairs. She was wearing one of his mother's best suits; a very expensive one in pale blue silk. He knew his mother would have asked her to wear it.

'You look lovely,' he said, helpless.

They stood in the doorway as Jack's parents came out of

the drawing-room together. The old man's voice was steady and polite.

'There can be no question of your living here together,' he said. 'I regret your action, Jack. However, I acknowledge that you are now man and wife.' He was unable to continue, but handed Jack a wallet of money.

'Conscience money!' Bridie had her mother's temper. Jack put his hand on her arm. He knew what it had cost his parents to do this.

'You will find an hotel,' his mother said, 'and you will be able to have a honeymoon. We would both like that for you. And when you return, you will have your own home to go to, and that is best.'

They didn't see them out, though they listened to the sound of Jack's bike as it roared off down the drive away from their house and off along the road that led to Derbyshire, and for a long time after the sound of it had died away they still imagined they could hear it, and didn't speak.

'And we called our first daughter Josephine, after my pa,' Grandpa Jack said. 'She sorted them out, all right. He thought the world of you, Josie.' My mum moved across so she was sitting next to him.

'Well,' said Granny Dorothy. 'It wasn't like that for me. I didn't have a mother to tell me I could or I couldn't. My dad was too busy working and that to think much about what I was up to. And Albert was the boy next door, or as good as. But I was like you, Jess. I was a bit of a dreamer, you see. I wanted a handsome prince .... '

3 The Buffer Girl

'There was a princess long ago
                    long ago, long ago
There was a princess long ago,
                    long ago.'

'Dolly! It's your turn!'

Louie Hooley pushed her little sister Dorothy into the middle of the ring of dancing children.

'Hide your eyes, Dolly! You mustn't see him coming!'

Six-year-old Dorothy pressed her grimy fingers against her eyelids and giggled. The children dancing on the cobbles round her were barefoot. She could hear the clap and swish of them swirling past her, and daren't look. She was in a red sea, with black shapes floating.

'She lived alone in a big high tower . . . .'

She could pick out Louie's voice, loud and shrill, here, and then there. She felt the air move as the dark shapes swept past.

'A wicked witch she cast a spell . . . .'

Old Mrs Beatty. They all knew that.

'A great big forest grew around . . . .'

There was a rush of air round her as the children thrust their arms up, high, and pressed in to her. She bent her head right down, right into the comfort of her skirts. She could hear someone galloping, galloping, with heavy boots, round the outside of the circle, round and round, coming for her. She started to sob; excited.

'A handsome prince came riding by
                    riding by, riding by
A handsome prince came riding by,
                    riding by.'

Oh let him be nice. Let him be nice.

'He cut the trees down with his sword . . . .'

All round her were shrieks of laughter as the children were felled by the arm of the handsome prince. Dolly sank down on to the cold cobbles, her hair loose round her, hiding her face.

'He woke the princess with a kiss . . . .'

And she was pulled up, hard, so her wrists hurt, and her fists were dragged down from her face and held back, and Albert Bradley, snotty-nosed and big-limbed bent down and kissed her full on the lips.

The children scattered away from them, shrieking.

'And everybody's happy now,
                    happy now, happy now . . .'

right down the street, and back up again, with Dorothy and Albert pulled along by them, hand in hand, till Mrs Beatty came out of their house wiping her hands on her skirts and shouted,

'Louie! Dorothy! You're wanted. Your mother's had her baby!'

'Everybody's happy now,
                    happy now, happy now . . .'

Dorothy looked out of the bedroom window and smiled. Her little brothers and sisters were down there somewhere. Any minute now her older sister Louie would come round and sweep all the little ones in with her from their game, and help Dorothy to get them ready for bed. Louie was twenty now and married to a dark, strange man called

Gilbert. In those days he cherished her. She lived two doors down in a cheerful mess of a house; she was a noisy, comfortable, happy girl, not a bit like Dorothy, who was quiet and timid, a born worrier, their father always said – but then Dorothy had the house to look after, and the little ones to see to. She'd only been fourteen when their mother had died in childbirth and since then their father had closed in on himself, tight and cold and silent, and she felt as if she'd lost him, too. He had little time for any of his children now. He paid Mrs Beatty next door to help Dorothy while he was at the steelworks. The old woman had been at the birth of all his children, and she'd laid out his wife for him. He liked to stay out drinking till the little ones were in bed. It was easier for him, that way. When he came in Dorothy would set about warming his meal for him, and he would watch her, saying nothing. She was too quiet for him; too like his wife. Once he stroked Dorothy's hair when she leaned over to him with his plate, and she looked up, startled. He'd forgotten how to touch his children.

He would have liked Dorothy to stay at home and keep his house clean for him, but Louie got her a job in the buffing shop where she worked, in one of the big cutlery firms in town. Their mother had worked there too, and old Mrs Beatty, in her time. Dorothy brought the stink of work home with her every day; she couldn't keep the smell of the buffing-shop out of her clothes and her skin and her hair. Her father had always hated that smell; and so did she.

Today was a special day for Dorothy. It was Saturday, February 26th, 1931. Dorothy was seventeen today. It was also the day of the cutlers' ball, when her firm was to hold its annual dance at the Cutlers' Hall in town. This year everyone who worked for the firm had been invited.

'It'll be a right birthday treat for you, Dolly!' Louie had

said. Her big awkward husband, Gilbert, had gladly given her leave to go without him, and she was grateful for that. She was going to find it hard enough to coax Dorothy to go, and to enjoy herself when she got there, without dragging Gilbert along too.

Dorothy had been cold with excitement all day. It was the first time she'd been to a dance of any sort. It was the first time she'd celebrated a birthday.

'Come on, Dolly, let's get you fettled!' Louie called up to her, and Dorothy ran downstairs to wash the muck of work off her hands and her face, and out of her long thick hair. She and Louie scrubbed each other down, and then Louie sat her in the hearth while she crimped her hair for her. They chattered away, full of it all, holding the curling tongs in the heat of the coals till they glowed, and then wrapping Dorothy's hair quickly round them.

'Hold it still,' Louie ordered. 'Don't wriggle or the lines will come out all wobbly.'

'You'll ruin that girl's hair,' Mrs Beatty warned. She was pressing their frocks. She held the iron near her face to feel its heat. Her spittle fizzed on it. 'It'll drop out before she's twenty-one, you'll see.'

'I don't care if it does drop out before she's twenty-one.' Louie's laugh was the sort that cracked inside your ear-hole. She could break bones in half with her voice. 'So long as it's all right for tonight, that's all.'

Mrs Beatty draped the hot dresses over the chair-back and settled down for a rest. She nagged on comfortably. 'When I was a girl it didn't do for young ladies to show their hair at all, never mind cook it.' But when old Mrs Beatty had been Dorothy's age the year had been 1876, and the world of young ladies then was a foreign land to them. 'I've seen more changes in my life-time than you're ever likely to see in yours, or would want to see, neither. Things have got wicked.' She purred into her cocoa and nodded off, missing the fun of seeing Dorothy put on her lisle stockings and the blue satin dress with red posies that she'd helped her to make.

The little ones crowded round for a good look at their sisters before they set off, and their clamour woke Mrs Beatty up again briefly. She had come to keep an eye on them while their widowed father was on night-shift at the steelworks, and to take advantage of a fire that she herself couldn't afford.

'You look bonny enough,' she murmured, and was asleep again before the girls had time to put on their powder. They slipped out into the street and ran arm in arm across the cobbles to where their friends were waiting for them at the tram stop.

The Cutlers' Hall was in Church Street, near the middle of town. Lights blazed from all its windows. Even from the street outside, with all its bustle of trams and traffic, you could hear the strains of the orchestra, and the babble of voices and laughter. Dorothy, shy, held on to her sister's arm as they went up the steps to the entrance hall. She gazed round at the black and green walls that gleamed like marble, the crystal chandeliers, the glowing polish of the woodwork; at the height of the pillars and the decorated ceiling, and at the broad sweep of the grand staircase that she was going to have to climb up if she was ever going to get near the ballroom. A woman in a pale green taffeta dress rustled down from the top flight on the arm of a young man and stood poised on the landing. She turned to smile at another group who were coming down to her, and the huge mirror behind her held her poised like one of the paintings round the walls. Her hair was permed in rows like the deep waves of the sea, in the newest fashion, and real jewels flashed at her throat.

'That's boss's wife,' Louie whispered. 'And that's boss's son, Mr Edward. In't he a peach!' She laughed loudly, in the shrieking way she had, and the party on the stairs turned their heads slightly towards them, and away again, and Dorothy blushed – not at her sister's coarseness, but because Mr Edward, son of the owner of one of the most famous cutlery firms in the world, had caught her eye and was staring coolly at her.

And she felt his eyes on her all evening, especially when she found herself laughing for joy at the dancing and singing to herself the tunes that she had only heard before in the singing at work. The little orchestra now filled them out with harmonies: *'Danny Boy'*, *'I'll Take You Home Again Kathleen'*, *'Roses are Blooming in Picardy'* . . . .

'I say,' whispered a voice in her ear. 'Did you know you're the prettiest girl here?'

'Am I?' She daren't turn her face to look at Mr Edward, even though his breath was warm on her cheek.

'You've eyes the colour of bluebells.'

She smiled at a plate of cakes on the buffet table.

'I'd like to ask you for the next dance,' he went on. 'And I shan't take no for an answer.'

She looked round for her friends, but they'd all gone off somewhere; smoking, or blotting their glowing cheeks with powder. Mr Edward put his hand on her shoulder and steered her out to the centre of the floor and she stood rigid with mortification while they waited for the music to start. She knew how to dance all right. Louie had seen to that, giving her lessons in the kitchen under the dripping clothes-rack while old Mrs Beatty hummed the tunes and tapped out the rhythm with her steel-tipped stick, and all her little brothers and sisters sat in their night-gowns on the kitchen bench to watch. She knew every dance there was to know, and was as light and lively on her feet as her mother had been. And Mr Edward could dance too. Now she knew that everyone's eyes were on her, and she didn't care. She wanted all the girls to notice her triumph. At the end of the dance his arms still held her and what's more his eyes held her too; and even though the music had stopped and all the other dancers were moving back to their seats she wanted that moment to hold her there for ever.

But, 'Edward! Edward!' his mother hissed at him, in a voice that was a shade too harsh for the smooth face under the permanent waves, and Mr Edward's firm grasp wilted.

'Wait for me after the ball,' he whispered. 'Will you?' Not looking at her but at his mother. 'Say you will.' And, 'I'll drive you home.'

'I'll drive you home!' Never had a motor-car been in Dorothy's street! At the end of the dance, when she was queuing with her sister for her coat and easing her feet out of her shoes, she told Louie that even though the last tram had gone she wouldn't be walking home with her.

'Mr Edward's taking me in his car,' she whispered.

'Don't be mad!' said Louie. 'Him, bring you home! Down Attercliffe, with me dad waiting to strap him for his cheek. Forget it, Dorothy. He's having you on.'

So arm in arm the sisters and their friends scuttled down from the scented ballroom and limped their blistered way home through the dark streets to Attercliffe.

But Dorothy couldn't forget Mr Edward that easily. That night she dreamt about him, and all next day too, when she was busy with the cooking and the housework, and she held a picture of herself with him, a still, coloured image like a painting, but with music in the background, and it showed him with his face bent down towards her at the end of the dance, and her with her face held up to his. When Albert Bradley from over the road lingered, as he always did, till Dorothy's father had gone to work, and knocked on her door for his morning kiss before racing down the street to clock on at the steelworks, he met with a fullness of lips that he'd never come across before.

'Why, Dolly, tha's coming on!' he said, stepping back for air, and Dorothy opened her eyes, shocked to think that Albert's blotched and bristly face should have put her in mind of Mr Edward.

'Get away with you, Albert Bradley,' she said, and he did, haring up the street to beat Dorothy's dad to the works gates, and grinning all day long at Dorothy's new magic.

Louie's strange husband, Gilbert, left for work at the same time, and she came round to Dorothy's house to help her to get the little ones up. Then they got ready for work together. They had to protect themselves from the gritty dust of the buffing wheel. They took newspapers from the pile that the neighbours brought round for them at the end of every week and tied sheets of them round each other – chest, arms, stomach, legs, till there was no clothing left to be seen except for the newly washed and daisy-white calico head-quares that they tied round their crimped hair. They collected their sandwiches, and left Mrs Beatty her penny for taking the little ones to school and back; and set off, rustling, for their tram, gathering their friends on the way. The girls chattered and shrieked and gossiped as the tram swayed down to town, and Dorothy gazed out at the houses with sunlight as pale as sand on their windows and thought of the rich gleam of chandeliers, and felt the warmth of Mr Edward's breath on her cheeks.

Much later that morning Mr Edward arrived at work. He'd had a bad weekend, dreaming about Dorothy. He was quite determined to find her again. All the people who had been to the ball had been employed by his father, so he knew that she would be in the building somewhere. He wouldn't let her slip away from him again, in her shyness.

In between inspecting the neat rows of boxed cutlery and candlesticks and meat plates that were lined up for export, he roamed from office to office and from floor to floor, anxious to get a glimpse of her; and Dorothy, standing all day long over her buffing wheel while clouds of black dust settled over her newspaper arms and body and her calico head-square, kept casting glances over her shoulder, sensing with every nerve that he was somewhere in the building and that he was looking for her. But it never occurred to him to look among the buffer girls, even though the sickly sweet metal-and-hot dust smell of their work lay heavy in every room, and the whirr of their machinery wound interminably through the day, and the lusty singing of the girls at their work chimed in every corner. If he had climbed up to the top floor of his father's building he would have seen the long buffing shop hot and bright with sunlight pouring through the roof windows, and the forty girls standing in their row putting the gleam on all those articles he inspected. They would be holding their faces away from the sand-dust that the wheel sprayed back at them, and from time to time they'd dash with their mugs to the tap in the corner and swill their mouths out, or they'd stretch back their shoulders to ease the ache, or flex the muscles of their feet.

'I'll take you home again, Kathleen' they'd be singing, or 'My old man, said follow the van, and don't dilly dally on the way . . . .' All day long they'd be singing, and from time to time the little one with eyes like bluebells in her blackened face would look over her shoulder for someone.

But at last it was clocking-off time. The machine stopped. The girls put out their pieces of holloware to be counted, and those with husbands' meals to cook and shopping to do on Attercliffe Common urged the ones who wanted to chat and dawdle to hurry up. They crowded out of the building together; newspaper arms and legs, faces, hands, calico head-squares, all as black as soot.

Dorothy clattered out behind the others, listening to their jokes and laughter and wrapped up still in her warm thoughts of the dance; and saw Mr Edward by the steps, dapper as a new sixpence and holding a posy of violets.

'For me!' she breathed.

His eyes flashed up and up the steps as the workers streamed out. Dorothy broke away from her sister to run to him, but Louie pulled her back.

'Don't,' she warned. 'He's never waiting for you.'

'He *is*,' said Dorothy, breaking free.

'Not *you*!' Louie's voice wailed.

Dorothy ran right up to Mr Edward, her newspapers flapping away from her arms. He had moved away as the top floor workers came down, and was about to give up his vigil.

'Mr Edward!'

He half turned, knowing the voice, and went back towards the steps. He had to push past the grimy blue-eyed girl on the pavement, and he brushed her dust off his coat in annoyance. The buffer girls yelled at Dorothy to hurry or they'd miss the tram; and, as she ran past him again, he realised that the girl he was looking for had vanished like the music and the lights and all the scents and laughter of the dance. He dropped the violets in the gutter and strode back to his car, and Louie, coming to hook Dorothy's arm in her own, bent down and picked them up for her kitchen table.

At the steelworks at the end of Dorothy's street Albert was about to finish his shift. He stood in the flare of heat as the great river of golden steel gushed down the channel into its mould. He would work here for the rest of his life, he knew that. And every night he would go back home to Dorothy. He thought of her morning kiss, and knew that he'd have to act fast before things got beyond his control. The furnace winked a white eye at him as the huge door was swung open and slammed shut again. He must go. Men shouted at him on their way past. His skin scorched with the heat, and still he couldn't move. He watched a massive rod of steel blaze white; red sparks from it spattered to the high, dark vault. He would ask her tonight.

He raced down to her house as soon as he'd clocked off. Dry as he was with the heat of the works, he didn't stop at the pub to slake his thirst as the other workers did. He reached Dorothy's door just as Mrs Beatty was coming out, and he hovered in the passage to let the old woman pass.

'You're early tonight, aren't you, Albert, for your kiss?'

'I've got special business tonight, Mrs Beatty.'

'Have you? What kind of business?'

'I'm going to pop her a question.'

Mrs Beatty chewed thoughtfully on the last bit of bread in her gums, and spat out the crusty bit that was annoying her. 'She's not in the mood for questions, Albert. I should come back tomorrow.'

'She's not poorly, is she?'

'She is.' Mrs Beatty pushed past him, sorry enough for the lad, but her back was hurting her. 'Not the sort of poorly you mean, though.'

'What sort of poorly?'

'Heart sort.' The old woman pushed open her door and went in for the night.

Dorothy heard Albert knocking but she lay in her bed with the candle out and not much of the day's grime washed off her face, except by tears.

'It's Albert, come for his kiss,' one of her sisters crept into the room to whisper to her. Dorothy bit her lip.

'Have I to tell him he can't have one tonight?'

'Yes. Tell him that.'

'Have I to tell him he can have one in the morning?'

'Tell him I'll see.'

The little sister passed on the message and then came up to creep into bed with her. Albert went home, ashamed.

'Dolly,' her sister whispered to her, much later, 'why are you crying?'

Dorothy sighed, and turned her head so that she could see out of her window to where the moonlight gleamed on the slate roof of Albert's house, and all down the terrace of slate roofs, and beyond that another street of slate roofs, and beyond that again another.

'I don't know, really,' she said. 'It's just that I'll never get away.' Never be posh, she thought. Never know where romance might lead me to.

'We don't want you to,' her sister said.

Dorothy watched, quiet, as the sky came to its full blackness and drained away again.

As soon as her father went out the next morning, Albert was at the door.

'Hello, Albert,' she said. 'It's you.'

He noticed how heavy her eyes were and decided to get on with it quick. 'Will you marry me, Dot?' he asked. Louie and Mrs Beatty were behind the door, listening. He knew that.

Dorothy sighed. 'All right.'

Albert tapped the step with his boot. Men hurried past on their way to work.

'Do you want a kiss this morning?'

'All right. But don't be late for work, will you, Albert Bradley? We want all the money we can get now, if we're to be wed.'

And she pushed her hair back and turned her face up to his, ready.

4 The Saturday Hop

My father, Michael, didn't take after my grandad Albert. No running off to work in the early hours of the morning for him. He hated work, though he always says it's because work hated him. Nothing ever seemed to go right for him. He was always in some sort of trouble. At home, if his little sister Maureen fell over or lost anything, or anything got broken, somehow it was always Michael's fault. Granny Dorothy was glad to get him off her hands and into the little local school, and it was the same story there. If a window was smashed Michael always happened to be standing near it at the time. If he went into the yard and found two lads fighting he got the blame. One of the last things he did before leaving school was to receive a mug for the coronation in 1953 and to drop it on the way home. Then he knew that not only were his parents, his sister, all the teachers at school and most of the local shopkeepers against him, but Queen Elizabeth the Second was as well.

His father got him a job at his own steelworks, labouring, and in a month he'd lost it for shouting at the foreman for picking on him. Albert said he was a disgrace to the family. Michael gave up then. He didn't even try to get another job. His mother was on the sick herself by that time, wheezing up a legacy of dust from her buffer girl days. She certainly couldn't be doing with him sprawled round all day. He used to sit and read American comics with his long legs stretched half-way across the room, right into the fire-place, and she could neither get round him nor over him to get on with her household chores. She used to shove him out if she could, soon after Maureen had gone off to work, and tell him not to come back until he'd found himself a job. 'You'll finish up a dirty old man with no stamps on your card,' she'd say. 'And then what'll become of you, Michael?'

'You'll see, Mum,' he'd say. 'I'll be leaving home soon enough, and I'll travel, all round the world. Then you'll be sorry. You'll miss me then, when I'm on the other side of the world.'

She'd shake her head and smile at him. 'You've got a lot to learn, Michael,' she'd say. 'A lot of growing up to do.'

He'd slam out of the house, angry at her, angry at himself, and make his way down to El Mambo's coffee bar and listen to the juke box. He was never on his own there. There were always plenty of other lads who didn't work, or wouldn't, or couldn't, and they'd all be there, drinking coffee and dreaming about better things.

'America, that's where we should be,' his friend Alan would say, cleaning his finger-nails with the teeth of his comb. 'Not Attercliffe.' Girls, they were after. Not jobs.

That was something else that Michael had never had any success with. Finding a girlfriend. Alan kept bringing girls down to El Mambo's to meet him, but they never liked him. He didn't like them either for that matter, though it would never have occurred to him to admit that. They didn't like him because he wasn't worth having, and that was that.

'I'm a freak of nature,' he'd say to his face in the mirror over the fireplace when no one else was at home. 'And I'm still wearing school clothes, and my trouser legs are too short. That's why they don't like me.'

Maureen tried to take him in hand. She managed to get him a job at the factory where she worked. It was only for an hour a day, sweeping up round the gardens, but it brought him in enough to buy himself some clothes. He wanted to be kitted up by his eighteenth birthday. He hid his new clothes in Alan's bicycle-shed, ready for the big day. He'd come out on parade, he'd be one of the lads, and he'd show himself off at the Saturday hop. He brought his jeans home one night when his mum was out at a whist drive and his dad was on night shift. They weren't right.

'Fill the bath up for me,' he told Maureen. They still hadn't a bathroom in their house. Maureen did as she was told while Michael made the fire. Her mother always filled the bath for Albert. That was the way things were done. When the bath was ready, Michael undid his shoes and took off his socks and stepped in. There he sat, fully dressed, steaming gently, and reading his comics by the firelight.

'What you doing that for?' asked Maureen.

'Shrinking my trousers,' he said. 'They're too flappy.'

'Your legs'll turn blue, you know,' she said. In a far corner she was discreetly painting her own legs with Bisto. Nylons were far too expensive.

They didn't share much, Michael and Maureen. Privately, she thought he was quite nice-looking but as lazy as a cat. He thought of her as a kid. All she ever did was clean her teeth.

As soon as he'd finished with the bath Michael left Maureen to empty it out and slopped down to Alan's in his soggy jeans. Alan was still having his tea and Michael dripped on the step while he talked to him.

'You can't come in here,' Alan's mother said. 'Look at you, you've got blue puddles all over my nice clean step.'

'I've come to see if you fancy going to the hop on Saturday,' he shouted to Alan. Alan winked at him.

'Course I am. An' I've fixed thee up wi' a smashin' bird for it, an' all. She's a right cracker.'

'You said that last time.' Mike took a shoe off and shook the blue water out of it, 'She was horrible, that last one. And she had nits nesting in that beehive hair-do. She can't have combed her hair for weeks.'

Alan came to the door with his plate and another fork for Mike.

'Well, this un's smart, I can promise thee. She's my new girl's best pal from work, and *she*'s a right little queen.'

'You mean you haven't even seen her!'

'Not exactly, no, but stop worrying. I tell thee. She's a right cracker.'

Mike helped himself to a chip. 'She'd better be,' he said. 'It's my birthday on Saturday.'

'I'll bring thee a paper hat to wear, then,' said Alan. 'It'd look smart with that new jacket tha's got.'

He didn't wake up till twelve on the day of his birthday. His mother brought him a cup of tea. She watched him while he slept, thinking how like Albert he was, and how much he frowned in his sleep, too. He wasn't a happy boy, she thought. It was a shame. Boys should be happy.

'Come on,' she said. 'Up.'

She sat and drank her own cup of tea while he dressed himself. Thin as a spider, she thought. 'What are you going to do to celebrate your birthday?' she asked.

'I'm going to the Saturday hop,' he said. 'With Alan.'

Dorothy didn't like Alan, but she kept quiet about it.

'I went to a dance on one of my birthdays,' she said. 'I think I was seventeen. I went to a ball.'

'Oh aye?' Mike combed his hair back into a quiff, like Alan's. 'Did you meet your handsome Prince Charming?'

'I did,' she said, mysterious, and he turned round to look at her, echoing her smile with his own.

'I bet you were the prettiest girl there,' he said rashly.

'I was,' she said.

She held her arms up, in a ballroom pose, and put her right hand in his, and her other hand on his waist.

'Hey, Mum, don't!' he squirmed.

She was miles away, 'Oh, how we danced, on the night, of the ball . . . ' she sang. 'Come on, Michael, pick your big feet up! La la, la la la, la la la . . . .'

'Mother! Leave off!' Laughing, he pushed away from her, and trod on his cup of tea.

He sat on the bed, head in his hands, while Dorothy picked the bits up. That was another thing. He didn't know how to dance.

That night he slipped out while his dad was in the middle of a row with Maureen. She had come downstairs in a new polka-dot skirt, rustling along in five or six stiff net petticoats. It wasn't easy for her to sneak out with all that noise going on but Mike couldn't resist making it harder for her. Actually he'd never seen her looking so pretty.

'Pooh,' he said. 'You smell like the allotments!'

'Shut up! It's Devonshire Violets!' she hissed. She tossed back her pony tail that showed off her slim white neck, and he saw that she had make-up on.

'Where are you off to, tarted up like that?'

That was what made Albert look up from his football pools and start shouting. He ordered her to scrub herself clean at the kitchen sink, and Dorothy rushed to the girl's defence and said she'd promised her she could stay out till the ten o'clock bus, and then Maureen burst into tears and said she'd never get a boyfriend at this rate, and that she was only going out with Barbara anyway, and in the hullaballoo that followed Mike crept out. He closed the door on the din and sauntered up the street in the evening sunshine. 'I'm glad I'm not a lass, anyroad.'

Down at the bike-shed Alan had his clothes ready for him. Bright pink socks, bootlace tie, blue shoes with two-inch crepe soles, and his newest prize, that he'd dreamed about for nine whole weeks – a pale blue drape jacket with a velvet collar.

'How do I look?' he squinted at himself in the mirror on Alan's handlebars.

'Oh, gi'e o'er,' said Alan. 'Come on, kid. We'll miss 'em.'

He set off at a running pace with Mike doing his best to keep up with him without spoiling the set of his brilliantined quiff. They were early at the meeting place, which gave him a chance to eye himself in the shop windows, and to do a few practice slouches.

'Lasses have come!' Alan said. 'Gi'e o'er preenin' thissen, tha great peacock!'

Mike could hear the quick clack of the girls' heels on the pavement, and their nervous giggles. He gave his bootlace a last tug and stuck his fists in his pockets out of the way. Alan elbowed him.

'What did I tell thee! A right pair of crackers. That little 'un's thas – lass in spotty frock.'

Mike turned, pale already, and looked down into the frightened face of his sister Maureen.

It was only because she wouldn't stop blowing her nose or running after him in her new clicky shoes, that Mike slowed his furious pace down the Moor and let her catch up with him.

'Stop roaring, Mo.'

'I can't help it. What can I do? Barbara's gone off to the hop with that Alan . . . . How can I go back home now, Mike, at this time, after all the trouble I had getting out and all? And I thought I was going out with a nice young man from Totley . . . .'

'Totley!'

'That's what Barbara told me. And it turns out to be you . . . and *you* turn out to be a Teddy-boy.' Her voice rose in a howl of disappointment. Mike looked round anxiously.

'Shut it, will you? How d'you think *I* feel? I was told I'd be dating a real little smasher. Aw heck – shut up!'

He swung off again, and she clicked after him. 'Tell you what,' he said at last. 'I'll take you into the hop, provided you don't tell any of the lads that you're my sister.'

'Thanks, Mike. And I won't tell Dad you've turned into a Ted, if you don't tell him that Barbara went off without me.'

The bargain was struck and they arrived at the Locarno, which was already throbbing with the sound of the band and the smell of sweaty bodies. The manager didn't like Teds, but he let them in because Maureen looked so worried and because Mike emptied his pockets willingly to show that he hadn't any flick-knives hidden. As soon as they were inside, Mike bought Maureen a glass of sarsparilla and told her to get lost till half-past nine. She spotted some of her friends from work and went over to the row of chairs that the girls sat in, down one side of the hall. Mike joined the row of lads on the opposite side and eyed up the talent. The lighting wasn't too good, but he spotted one that he fancied, a little clean-looking girl with a dark pony-tail, bit like Maureen, really. He sauntered across to her when the band struck up again and wandered up and down in front of her for a bit, giving her a chance to notice him; and also tuning in to the conversation she was having with her friends – waiting for his moment.

'I see you're wearing your pointed bra,' said one.

'They're uncomfortable, aren't they, but you have to wear one here.'

'You know what happened to me last week, don't you?' his girl said. 'I were dancing with this feller, and we got into a right tight clinch in the quickstep, and when the dance finished, guess what?'

'What, Jennifer?'

'There were two dints in his jumper where the points of my bra had gone in. And guess what?'

'What?'

'I'd gone right flat! I had to go off to the Ladies' and push my points out again.'

The girls babbled on. Mike grinned. Jennifer. She'd do.

'Er . . . excuse me,' he said.

The girls froze.

'D'you want this dance?'

They turned away. Jennifer cast him half a smile. Mike hated this bit. His collar was too tight all of a sudden. His hands were too big. His socks were too bright. His spots blazed.

'Come on. It's a nice one, this.'

Jennifer looked past him. 'I'm with Lucy.'

Her friend bent down and picked up her handbag. 'Don't bother about me, I'm sweating. I was just going to powder my nose, anyway.'

Jennifer shook her head at her. 'I'm not dancing with him,' she mouthed, wrinkling her nose. Mike gave her back her half-smile and slouched back to the lads' side.

'She wasn't my type,' he told Alan.

He stood, glum, watching the couples dancing, wondering why he bothered putting himself through this misery. 'I can't see what all the fuss is about,' he thought. Alan's partner, Barbara, had gone off with a clean lad in a suit, but it didn't seem to bother Alan. He seemed to be able to dance with any girl he picked on. It was easy for him. Mike had a bit of a cold still from wandering round in wet trousers the other day; he wondered if that had anything to do with it. The girls were like flowers in their bright dresses and perfume, tantalising and confusing with their smiles. He thought of himself suddenly as a little boy, trapping butterflies in his fist and holding them there till their wings stopped fluttering; and of the cold kind of horror he had felt when he let them drop from his hand, wishing they'd dance again.

But here he was with an itchy cold-sore, trapped in a game he didn't know how to play, and still, in his heart of hearts, wanting to dance with Jennifer. He was just about to stroll across to her side and try again when he was distracted by a sudden commotion up at the other end of the room, near the band. The girls rushed over to join a ring of spectators. Jennifer turned her head; obviously, Mike thought, to see if he was coming, and he risked a wink at her. She giggled something to her friend.

'I'm all right here,' Mike thought. 'I'm sure I am. Perhaps she'll let me buy her a glass of pop in a bit. I won't rush it, though.'

Then he saw that Alan was lying on the floor wrapped round a lad in a leather jacket and that Barbara was blowing her nose and being comforted by Maureen. This was a bit more like it!

'Come on, Alan!' he shouted, proud of his friend. The manager and another large man picked up the two fighters as if they were no heavier than a couple of cats and dragged them right across the dance floor and out through the doors at the far end. Barbara ran after them, blushing to the roots of her hair, and Maureen clicked after her, carrying both their handbags. The band played on but nobody moved. They were all straining to catch what was being said behind the doors. Then the lad in the new suit who'd been dancing with Maureen earlier on dashed out and came back in with her, and everyone sighed.

Mike decided he'd better tell Jennifer that Maureen was his sister, in case she'd seen them coming in together. It wouldn't do to let her think he'd been jilted. He felt a hand on his shoulder.

'And you can get out, an' all,' the manager said to him. Everyone turned, interested.

'Me! I haven't done owt!'

'I'm sick of Teds. I don't like Teds. I'm not having any more Teds in here.'

'But I'm not with him. I don't even know him!'

'I told you. Out!'

'It's the first time I've worn this jacket.'

'Out.'

'I've got to see my sister home.'

'Now. One ... two ... .'

Mike soon caught up with Alan. 'I couldn't let you go home on your own,' he panted. 'I'd just got myself fixed up with a smashing bird, too.'

He changed back into his old clothes in Alan's shed. Alan had got blood all down his jacket.

'D'you think tha Maureen'll wash that off for me?' he asked, dabbing his nose.

'Course she will,' Mike promised. 'No trouble.'

He trudged back home, too fed up even to call in for some chips on the way. As he passed his kitchen window he saw his dad's head bob up from reading the paper and he groaned to himself. 'More rows!' He kicked the bin on his way past it. But his dad came right to the door to meet him, beaming, and slapped him on the back. 'I'm glad you got back before I slipped out for my pint, Michael,' he said. 'There was a letter for you this morning, and I clean forgot to give it you with Maureen's carrying on. Here y'are. Open it up, then. It's full of good news.'

Mike took the brown envelope from him and turned it over delicately. 'Have you been drinking or something?'

'No, I tell you, I was on my way out. Tell you what, when you've read this, I'll take you down for a pint. You deserve it.' Albert laughed again, full of himself.

'What's the big joke, Dad?'

'No joke. Open your letter.'

'You seem to know all about it. Have you been reading it or summat?' Mike still couldn't bring himself to open it. He wasn't used to getting letters. His dad took it off him and ripped it open.

'Course I know all about it. I've been expecting this coming for weeks, and so've you. It's your call-up papers.'

Mike sat down, feeling ill. 'Call-up? National Service?'

How could he have forgotten that? All the lads went into the forces at eighteen – it had been on his mind since he left school. And now, today of all days, it had come. Some birthday present! Her Majesty's Services. Good old Queen Elizabeth the Second!

'I don't want to go into the army,' he muttered. Don't want to go away from home. Don't want to get hurt.

'It'll make a man of you, you'll see!' said Albert. 'Come on, Michael, don't look so miserable, this is a big day for you. And for us, eh, Dolly? We'll have him off our hands at last!' He thumped him across the back again, a bit too hard, his voice a bit too loud for joking. 'Let's go and have a pint on it.'

But Michael felt more like crying than celebrating. He didn't want to be a man yet. He wanted to have a bit of fun first.

He looked across to his mother for support.

'You have to go, and that's that,' she said. 'You'll look nice with your hair cut.'

He fingered his quiff, miserable.

'And that uniform will suit you. You always said you wanted to travel, love.'

Albert went off to the pub on his own, and Dorothy took the papers out of Mike's hands, folded them back into the envelope, and stuck them behind the clock on the mantelpiece. She made him a cup of cocoa. He took it up to his room, and while it was cooling he took down all his model planes and put them in a carton for Alan's little brother. He lay in bed listening to his mother moving round setting the table for breakfast, and making her own way to bed. He heard Maureen clicking up the street, and soft footsteps following her down the passage. He prised open the window and listened to her giggling.

'I can hear you snogging!' he shouted.

Her footsteps clicked into the kitchen, and her young

man ran off up the street. Albert came home, and Mike heard their low voices murmuring as Maureen made him a drink and told him about the hop.

He lay for a long time, listening to the house sounds settling down, and the tom-cats yowling along the yard walls. He hid his face under his pillow, and when at last he fell asleep he dreamed that Jennifer had danced with him.

'I did feel sorry for you in those days, Michael,' Granny Dorothy laughed. 'You were so thin and long and miserable! You didn't know a thing about life. Not a thing.'

'Did you ever see Jennifer again?' I asked.

Dad winked at my mum. 'Many a time,' he said. 'Still do, don't I, Josie? I owe a lot to Jennifer. But I think I owe even more to Lucy Cragwell . . . .'

5 Lucy Cragwell

Jennifer had been to the Saturday hop with some friends from work. Among them had been Lucy Cragwell, a lumpish, sniffy girl who worked on the cash-till in the canteen. She had invited her to come on impulse, because she felt sorry for her. She'd found her crying in the toilets that day; not just having a little weep the way most of the girls did from time to time, but really sobbing, white and hysterical, great belly-sobs of misery. Jennifer stood, embarrassed, with a comforting hand on her shoulder, while Lucy heaved up her grief.

'Lucy? Lucy, what's the matter?'

'I wish . . . I was . . . . pretty. I . . . . hate . . . being ugly . . . Jennifer.'

And there it was, Lucy's agony laid at her feet like bad news that's just come through the letter-box. One minute it had nothing to do with her. The next minute it was hers to cope with.

'Of course you're not ugly.'

'Of . . . course I am. Look at me.'

Lucy scraped her thin, straight, and tear-wet hair away from her face and tucked it behind her ears. She and Jennifer inspected the white moon face in the mirror, the eyes red and blotched with unhappiness, the thin slit of a mouth. Behind her, Jennifer's hair bushed out, lustrous, her skin bright with health, her eyes dark with sympathy.

'It's only because you've been crying, Lucy.'

Shudders of unhappiness shook the girl again. 'It isn't fair. Look at you, and . . . look at . . . me. My mother says I shouldn't mind being ugly, as long as people like me. But people *don't* like me.'

It was true. Nobody liked Lucy Cragwell much. She was plain and she was sniffy and she smelt a bit, she always looked miserable, and she always would do. She was only seventeen. Jennifer didn't know what to say.

'Some of us are going to the dance at the Locarno tonight, Lucy. Would you like to come?'

Lucy drew in her breath sharply.

'The girls don't like me. They wouldn't want me to go.'

'I want you to go. We're meeting outside at eight o'clock. Try and come.'

Jennifer went back to her office, glad that she wasn't ugly, and that she'd been able to say something to cheer Lucy up, and quite sure that she wouldn't come.

But Lucy did come. When the girls arrived she was already there, slopping backwards and forwards in her mother's shoes and in a dress she'd worn to the Christmas social, stained as it had been then with toothpaste. The girls giggled to each other when they saw her but Lucy was used to that.

'Shut up,' Jennifer said to them. 'Come on, Lucy. You come in with me.'

Lucy followed her in, her loose shoes clattering, and sat slightly apart from them, grateful and quiet, through the evening. She saw Mike and Maureen come in together, and she watched Mike all evening. She flushed deeply when he came across to ask Jennifer to dance, and when he was turned down. 'I'll dance with you,' she wanted to say, but daren't.

And that night, while Mike dreamed of Jennifer, Lucy Cragwell dreamed of Mike Bradley.

Next Monday, in the canteen, she leaned across to Jennifer as she approached the cash desk with her dinner tray. Jennifer could smell her fishy breath.

'You know Maureen Bradley?' she asked.

Jennifer didn't know her. Lucy pointed her out, sitting

by herself near the window. 'I remember her now,' said Jennifer. 'She was at the hop, wasn't she, in a polka-dot skirt?'

'Do us a favour,' Lucy breathed. 'Ask her who that Teddy-boy was who came in with her.' Her neck and her ears were scarlet with embarrassment.

'Why, Lucy? D'you fancy him?'

Lucy hung her head. Her pale strands of hair fell forward into Jennifer's soup. 'Sort of,' she whispered.

'I'll see what I can do,' Jennifer promised. She took her tray over to Maureen's table. 'You know that Teddy-boy who came to the dance with you last Saturday?' she asked.

Maureen sighed. 'He's nothing to do with me. He's only my brother.'

Jennifer laughed in sympathy. 'What's his name, though?'

'Michael. Why?'

'Oh, no reason. I'm only asking for a friend.' She watched Lucy at the cash-desk. Her pale moon face floated in space over the trays of food. Jennifer felt a sudden rush of warmth for her. 'Could you do me a favour, Maureen? Could you ask your Michael to come in here tomorrow and *buy* something from the canteen?'

'*Our Mike?*'

'Could you? Please?'

Maureen couldn't wait to get home that night and tell Mike that Jennifer wanted a date with him.

He stared at her. 'Who's Jennifer?' he asked. His heart leapt like a frog in his shirt.

'You know very well who Jennifer is. You never took your eyes off her the other night at the Locarno. I saw you.'

'Oh,' he nodded thoughtfully. 'That Jennifer.'

He rushed round to tell Alan. 'I've got a date,' he panted. 'That girl at the dance wants to see me.'

Alan was squatting over a bowl of water, trying to find a

puncture in his bike tyre. He wasn't as excited as Mike. 'Chase no bird,' he warned him, not looking up.

'I'm not chasing her. She's chasing me.'

'I'm warning thee. Chase a bird and she'll fly away.' He sighed as the bubbles floated up, and lifted the tyre carefully out of the bowl. 'If she wants to see thee, play hard to get. Let her see thee wi' some other bird. Keep her guessing.'

'Aw, come off it, Alan. I've only got a week before I go into the army.'

'Who gets the birds round here?'

'You do, Alan.'

'Right. Do as I say then. Chase no bird.'

Next day, nervous, Mike sauntered into the works canteen. He got himself a cup of tea and stood in front of Lucy, waiting to pay for it. She didn't notice him at first, as she was furtively finishing off a jam sponge that someone had left on a plate. When she looked up the tell-tale scarlet flashed across her neck. She couldn't swallow her mouthful of cake.

'I never thought I'd see you again!' she attempted on impulse, spraying crumbs at him. He couldn't grasp what she'd said but smiled at her and went to sit near the door. Jennifer was nowhere in sight. He sat for thirty minutes while Lucy hummed round him cleaning the tables, even though it wasn't her job, smiling pike-like at him and everyone else who came near her. Mike watched her moodily. At last he gave Jennifer up. He wandered towards the exit door. Lucy dodged after him.

'Bye!' she called sweetly.

'Cheerio.' He slammed the door behind him, and there was Jennifer.

'Hello,' he said, calm. 'I came.'

'So I see.'

She smiled at him. He looked better in normal working clothes, even if he was wearing old school trousers.

'Aren't you going to talk?' he said, smiling back foolishly.

'I'm due back at work now.'

'I can come tomorrow.'

'Good,' she said.

Good! He watched her walk down the corridor to the stairs that led to her office, and somehow moved himself out of the building into the yard. He could be seen by several office girls and by Lucy Cragwell from the canteen, leaping over benches, crazy as a bat.

Lucy nibbled cold chips and hummed to herself.

The next day the same thing happened. Mike sat, fretful and disappointed, waiting for Jennifer, while Lucy wiped tabletops and sang. She was working out opening sentences in her head. Mike's anger mounted. Someone was trying to make a fool of him. At last he made his mind up. He would go. He swung out of the canteen and Lucy, desperate, dropped her dishcloth and slopped after him. Mike dodged away from her and ran away from the exit door and towards the offices. He would find Jennifer and make her tell him what it was all about. Heavy footsteps echoed in his wake. He saw Maureen and grabbed her arm.

'That girl's following me,' he said.

'So what? You're not scared of Lucy Cragwell, are you?' Maureen giggled. She slowed down to allow Lucy to catch up with them.

Girls were passing, high-voiced, laughing, all with their eyes on him, Mike thought. 'She's driving me crackers,' he said. 'She's following me round like a piece of toffee-paper stuck to me boot. Call her off, Maureen.'

His sister ducked out of the way as Lucy reached them, breathless, and hung laughing on to Mike's arm. The corridors were full of girls going back to their offices. Jennifer would be there any minute.

Lucy lifted her moon face up towards him, grabbing her

chance. 'Would you like to go to the pictures tonight?' she asked.

'Good,' he said, absently. He'd seen Jennifer. 'Great.'

'I know girls don't ask boys, but I think that's daft, don't you?'

'What? Yes.' Jennifer was only yards away. She must have seen him.

'So will you come? Will you?'

If he could just get away from her he might be able to reach Jennifer before she went up the stairs. He panicked. He remembered what Alan had said. He unwrapped Lucy's arm from his. 'Yes,' he said.

Lucy caught him again. 'Jennifer!' she shouted, loud enough for everyone in the building to hear. 'Mike and I are going to the pictures tonight.'

In the sea of laughing faces he focussed on Jennifer's, and couldn't make out anything at all from the look she gave him. But then, as he thought later, head in hands on the bench in the yard, he must have looked pretty blank too.

He didn't know what to do about that night. He'd never been asked out by a girl before. That was something, he supposed. But Lucy Cragwell! If he didn't turn up Jennifer might get to hear of it and think badly of him. Perhaps it was a kind of test. But what if it wasn't? He'd think badly of himself, he knew, if he let Lucy down. He had a picture of her, sniffy and lumpish by the works gates, waiting. Perhaps it was a joke, and Lucy would metamorphose into Jennifer when he arrived. Perhaps she wouldn't, and Alan would see them together, and laugh. He could tell Alan he was taking his advice after all. It might work. It might make Jennifer jealous. It wasn't worth the risk of not turning up.

He wore his Teddy-boy outfit. She was waiting for him when he arrived.

'I shouldn't really have come out tonight,' he told her.

'I've got packing to do. I'm going into the army.' Maybe she'd release him.

'I like soldiers,' she said, placid.

He walked slightly behind her on the way to the pictures, and insisted on paying for himself. During the film she slid her hand across and placed it in his own; a fish hand, clammy with cold. His skin prickled. When the film ended she stood waiting for him to put her coat on, and he caught the sharp smell of her sweat as she lifted up her arms.

'It's been the best night of my life, Michael,' she said, clopping awkwardly at his side in her borrowed shoes. 'I'll let you into a secret,' she went on. 'It's my very first date.'

His heart stirred with something like misery and something like pride. 'Mine too,' he said thickly.

He couldn't face the canteen the next day. Nor could he face the thought of not seeing Jennifer. He had to explain about Lucy. In the lunch-break he wandered round from the gardeners' shed and sat on the bench in the yard. The sky was low and yellow. No one sat out on days like this. Fat rain began to burst round him. He sat on, miserable and damp, watching the puddles grow and the dark wet stains spread across the bench. He knew Lucy was standing at the canteen window, watching him. He dipped his finger into a bolt-hole full of rainwater on the bench. 'J' he wrote carefully on the arm of the bench. He dipped again. 'E' 'N' .... She came out, holding up a pale blue umbrella. He'd wished her there, and she'd come. He put his hand over the letters.

'Jennifer,' he said. 'Will you come to the pictures tonight?'

Now he was conscious of the rain dribbling down the back of his neck.

'Must have been a good film if you want to see it twice.'

'I want to see it with you.'

'I should think you've got enough on your hands with Lucy Cragwell.'

'I didn't mean to take her out. Honestly.' Rain tipped from the umbrella and splashed on to his face as he stood up. 'It was an accident.'

'I suppose you did it for a dare.'

'Yes. No. Not a dare. Why should I do it for a dare?'

'A joke, then.' She shook her umbrella again, just missing his eye. 'Well, let me tell you something, Michael or whatever your name is –.'

'Michael,' he said. 'Mike . . . .'

'And this isn't a joke. Lucy Cragwell's in love with you.'

'What!' Oh no! 'Love!' Heck.

Lucy Cragwell, slow pike's smile hooked on him from the window. Arms bulging from her tight sleeves. Grey eyes flat as fishes. Humming with happiness.

'Oh no!'

'I can't stand lads like you,' Jennifer went on. 'She can't help it.'

'Neither can I,' said Mike. 'I can't help it.'

'I hope you're satisfied, that's all.'

Jennifer clicked away and Mike sank back on to the bench, tense and miserable and soaked to the skin by now. At last he stood up to go, and as he did so there was a tap on the canteen window and he turned to see Lucy waving at him. He groaned and turned away but within minutes he heard the slap of fat feet on the wet pavement and he knew that she was following him.

'How did you know it was my half day, Mike?' she said, steadying herself against him as she put her shoes back on; pleased with herself, pleased with him, and pleased with the rain that would make it necessary for her to hold her umbrella over them both.

'I didn't,' he said. 'It's just my luck.'

'Our luck,' she said. 'Do you want to come home with me for a cup of tea? This is my bus.'

He shrugged. He was too wet to care. He wanted to go home and write a letter to Jennifer; a poem, maybe. He wanted to get on with his packing. He wanted to write a will, donating his records and his Teddy-boy suit to an orphanage in case anything happened to him in the army. He wanted to float away in the rain and trickle down a grid in some quiet gutter.

He followed her on to the bus and off it again and into a dark little house that smelt of dogs. A large, plain woman, an older Lucy, came out of the kitchen to meet them. She looked at them both with distaste.

'Mum. This is Michael. I've told you about him,' said Lucy happily.

Her mother sniffed in a familiar way and sent her upstairs to change into dry clothes. Mike could hear her singing in a surprisingly sweet voice as she padded about in her room making the light fittings shake. Mrs Cragwell gave Mike a cup of tea as he steamed by the fire. He didn't like to sit down. A dog scratched and whined at the closed door. Lucy's mother bit a hard biscuit and glared at Mike. Her hair, grey and greasy, hung limp around her ears, and as Mike swallowed his first mouthful of tea he saw one of these same grey hairs unwind from the inside of his cup, and he felt it wrap itself round his tonsils. He tried to cough it up. Mrs. Cragwell cracked another bite of biscuit.

'You look after that girl, d'you hear me?' she said at last. 'I don't want any fooling around.'

Mike folded his tongue backwards in search of the hair.

'I've had my heart broke once and I don't want it happening to my daughter.'

He hooked his finger down the side of his mouth. His cup and saucer rattled in his free hand, spilling their contents.

'She's not pretty, and she's not clever,' Mrs. Cragwell said. 'But she's a good girl. Don't you hurt that girl's feelings.' Her eyes darkened with memories of her own sorrow. 'What's the matter with you? You got toothache?'

'I think I've swallowed something, Mrs Cragwell.'

'Cough it up, then.' She padded across the carpet and thumped his back. 'I must have dropped a bit of my ginger biscuit into your tea. Want one?'

All Mike wanted was to get out, but he didn't know how. He dived for the door as soon as he heard Lucy coming down the stairs.

'I've got to go now, and do my packing,' he said.

He saw Lucy's disappointed face. She'd put new clothes on, and make-up. She'd brushed her hair till it floated. She smelt of talcum powder.

'Don't go,' she said.

'No, really. I must. I'm lovely and dry now. Look. That side is anyway.'

'Can I see you tomorrow, Mike?'

'Of course. Yes. Why not?' Not much to offer in exchange for fresh air and rain, cold as broken promises and loneliness and lies. Tomorrow was his last day. His last chance to see Jennifer again.

'After work, then?'

And he was out, running this time, collar up, straight through puddles, head spinning.

Lucy Cragwell's in love with you. Don't hurt the girl. Don't go.

'Oh Lucy, Lucy,' Mrs Cragwell sighed, and put the kettle on for another cup of tea.

Mike's mother, Dorothy, had been shopping in town, getting things ready for him to take away. 'I've got you some nice new socks and underpants,' she said, trying to cheer him up at tea-time.

'He won't need those, Dorothy. The army will give him those,' Albert said with relish.

Mike sat hunched over his tea.

'Come on, Michael. Eat up.'

'He's in love,' said Maureen.

'Shut up, will you!'

'I thought as much,' Dorothy said, pleased. 'Not eating, staying up all hours, pacing round his room at night, coming home soaked through. I knew it.

'I am *not in love*.' Mike stood up. He was taller than his father, even.

'Her name's Lucy Cragwell, and she's foul,' said Maureen.

'She is *not foul*.'

'All right,' said Albert, recognising himself in his son for the first time, and sorry for him. 'We'll have no more of this. Eat the tea your mother's cooked for you, Michael. It's one of the last decent meals you'll get.'

Mike could be heard pacing round his room that night. He had his windows wide open. The curtains tugged against the hooks he used to hang his model planes on. Tomorrow he was leaving home, and when he came back he'd be a man. It was going to happen and there was nothing he could do to stop it and nobody cared. He wouldn't mind so much if somebody cared, but nobody did. If he had a girl to write home to, and a photograph of her to stick by his bed, and a promise to see him during leave, he wouldn't mind going. Jennifer would have done fine. But it looked as if it was going to have to be Lucy, unless he did something terrible to break her heart, and he didn't know how to do that.

'Poor old Lucy,' he thought, surprised. 'She's all right, really.'

Perhaps she would do.

When he stood outside the works gates the next day the first person he saw was Jennifer. He could smell her lily-of-the-valley perfume as she came up to him.

'Jennifer,' he said, desperate. 'I've got to talk to you. I'm going away tomorrow.

'I know,' she said. 'The army's going to make a man of you.'

'I *am* a man,' he said. 'I shave nearly every day now.'

'Well,' she smiled. 'You must be, then. Have a good time.'

She moved away. 'Wait,' he said. 'Could I write to you?'

Jennifer pouted, thinking hard. Lucy was coming. When she saw Mike she started running to him. Jennifer leaned forward and patted his arm. 'I'm too old for pen-pals,' she said. 'Anyway, I don't like Teddy-boys. You never hear of Teddy-*men*, do you?' She stood away again as Lucy panted up to them. 'I'll leave you two alone.'

Mike plunged his hands so deep into his pockets that he felt the lining rip. Lucy waited.

'Come on,' he said at last, and she plodded after him. Alan went past on his bike, jeering. 'If a cat got in my way I'd kick it,' Mike thought. 'No, I wouldn't. How could I kick a cat? I couldn't even squash a tadpole.' He had a sudden picture of himself in army uniform, a soldier, running at sandbags, screeching, plunging bayonets in. He moaned and reeled against the wall, hugging himself.

'You got that toothache again?' Lucy asked.

'I don't want to go in the army, Lucy.'

'You'll be all right.'

'I won't. I don't want to be a soldier. What's it all for? Killing people.'

'You'll make some nice friends.'

'I'm scared, Lucy.'

She looked at him thoughtfully. 'Course you are. I think I'd be scared, too. I'm glad girls don't have to go. It's not fair, I suppose, but I'm glad anyway.'

'You'll write to me, won't you?' All of a sudden he wanted the comfort of her plump arms round him. She put her cold hand on his and led him into a shop dorrway. She put her handbag down on the tiled floor and lifted her arms up on to his shoulders, turning her moon face up towards him.

'What's up?' he asked, worried.

'I want to give you a kiss,' she said. 'But I can't reach. You'll have to bend down.'

He bent down and allowed her thin slit of a mouth to rest against his. His head was reeling. I don't want to hurt her feelings, let her down, break her heart, he thought. I'm the only chance she's got.

'Now then,' she said, picking her bag up and stepping away from him. 'Just listen. I'm not going to write to you.'

Oh well, he thought.

'I know what you're thinking. You're thinking I'll do because there's no one else. You're thinking you'll keep me on because you don't want to hurt my feelings. You're sorry for me. You know I'll still be here when you come home on leave because no one else will have me. Shut up, I'm talking.'

Mike stared at the leaves edging round in the doorway. His throat was tight and swollen.

'I thought you were interested in me but now I know it's Jennifer you're after. Of course I knew that all along but I've been pretending. Shut up. I'm not that bothered. We could go on and on like this, with you feeling sorry for me and me trotting round after you because I'm scared of not getting anyone else, for years and years, d'you know that? We could end up getting married, Michael. Have you thought of that? What are you sniffing for? I'm the one who sniffs round here. We could end up with a string of kids who all had long bendy legs like you and fishy cod faces like me, have you thought of that? Well, I have. As a matter of fact, Michael Bradley, I've thought of nothing else since last Saturday night. And I've decided I don't want it. I don't want a bendy cowardy boyfriend who's too scared to admit that he doesn't even like me.'

'I do like you.'

'Shut up. I don't think I want anyone, actually. But if I ever do have someone it's going to be equal and fair and obvious from the start. Not him chasing me the way you chase Jennifer, (the way every lad in the works chases Jennifer, by the way.) And not me chasing him the way I've been chasing you. What a stupid way to carry on. That's what I think about love. If it isn't equal, it isn't real. And if it isn't real, then it isn't worth having. I'm catching that bus.'

That night Mrs Cragwell plodded upstairs with a cup of tea for Lucy. She didn't put the light on.

'Feeling better, love?' she asked.

Lucy sniffed. 'A bit.'

Mrs. Cragwell went over to draw the curtains. She could just make out a very tall, thin lad outside, his face white and child-like in the light of the street lamp. He'd been there since teatime. Mrs Cragwell shook her head, closed the curtains, and took Lucy's empty cup down to be washed.

Albert and Dorothy came down to the station to see Mike off the next morning. They were as anxious as he was, and shouted last-minute fondnesses to him. They'd got a lodger ready to move into his room that night, but they hadn't told him yet. Mike lifted his bag up onto the rack and leaned out of the window, excited suddenly. Billows of sooty steam gushed from the engine. Right along the platform doors were being slammed. The train shrieked. The porter stood with his flag poised.

'Wait! One more! Please wait!'

It was Jennifer, running along the platform, shouting and waving, with a small group of people running after her.

'Here, Jennifer! Here! I'm in here!' He pushed open the door. Jennifer saw him and grabbed the girl who was running behind her and shoved her into Michael's compartment.

'This is Michael Bradley,' she panted. 'This is my big sister, Josie. Phew!' she gasped, as her parents, Bridie and Jack, joined her on the platform. 'She's going to college,

Michael. He's going into the army, Josie. Phew!'

'Write to us!' Jack and Bridie shouted.

'Have a lovely time, Michael,' Dorothy and Albert said.

'I've heard about you,' said Josie. 'Jennifer's told me all about you.'

'Has she?'

The train lurched forward. The families yelled goodbye and Mike and Josie leaned out of the window together, and with a huge gasp the train heaved itself into speed. Steam swirled round the platform, hiding their families, and still Mike and Josie waved.

'It's a bit frightening, leaving home,' said Josie.

'No, it isn't,' Mike reassured her. 'Yes, it is, a bit. I didn't want to go at first. I'm glad now. Watch your head, there might be a tunnel.' He drew her back in.

'You've got a smut on your nose,' she said kindly.

'You're not a bit like Jennifer,' he said.

'I know I'm not. She's the pretty one who goes out dancing. I'm the quiet one who stays at home studying. I want to be a teacher.'

'You're nearly as pretty as she is,' Mike said. 'No, you're not. I mean ... sort of ... you *are* ... .'

The train rushed them into a tunnel. He sat in the blackness, bewildered. He could hear her snuffling. 'Different ... but just as nice. Nicer ... ' he tried. Her snuffling turned into a snort, and another; gasping snorts that she was trying to hold back but couldn't, and he felt the same nervous snorts rising up in him, and the more he tried to choke them back the more they burst out. Giggle bubbles, bouncing off each other in the blackness, exploding into wild shrieks that could be heard from one end of the tunnel to the other as the train plunged them away from Sheffield and into the new life that they would come to share.

6 Danny

Mike and Josie were married about three years later. It was always a very equal marriage. She was clever and thoughtful with occasional quick bursts of her mother's temper, which kept him in his place, or so Bridie, her mother, maintained. He was a very tall, healthy man. Neither of them can actually remember proposing to the other; they always knew they'd get married somehow. Their first child was a boy; he was born at home, and Bridie was there to help. It wasn't an easy birth; Josie went in and out of consciousness while it was going on, and Bridie kept bullying her to get on with the job. When at last he was born Bridie made the sign of the cross over him.

'What did you do that for?' asked Josie, chilled in her weakness, and Bridie only shook her head. 'He's a beautiful boy,' she said. 'Bless him.'

They called him Danny. It was Danny, more than anyone, who brought the families together. I was born when he was seven years old, and by then the truth about him had long since dawned. Bridie had seen it first and then Josie had guessed it and held the knowledge deep inside herself till Mike, too, saw it. Danny was only a few months old, lying on the bed to be dried after his bath, and Mike said, dry with sudden dread:

'He's got a funny way of kicking.'

'I know,' said Josie, quiet.

'He doesn't kick properly, does he?'

'No.'

Mike's fear made him angry. 'So what do you know that I don't?'

'Nothing, Mike,' she said. 'I don't know why he's like this. I just know he's different, and now you know, too. Don't ask me what it is.'

'Then we'll have to find out, won't we?'

That began a long series of visits to doctors and hospitals, operations for Baby Danny, and the slow understanding that he was never going to get better, that he would never walk properly, or play with other children; that he would become worse and worse over the years; and that he would never grow to be a man.

'All we can do for him is to make his short life more comfortable,' the specialist told Mike and Josie. 'There's no cure for this.'

When Danny was asleep Mike would sit by his cot, stroking and stroking his hair, and Josie would stand staring out of the kitchen window for hours at an end, till you would think that she would see leaves uncurl from their buds.

'I'm not strong enough for this,' she told Mike.

'You are,' he promised. 'We are.'

Danny was given his first wheelchair soon after his sixth birthday. He thought it was wonderful. Josie had taken him for his regular check-up at the Children's Hospital; she always carried him about straddled over her hip when he was too tired to walk. They left the hospital that day with the wheelchair, and she took him over the road in it to the park. They were to meet Mike there after work for a picnic. For the first time people started looking at Josie and Danny. When he'd been in a push-chair he was just like any other toddler. When she'd carried him on her hip he was just a tired child. Now people knew he was different, and their averted glances showed it.

Blind with unhappiness, while Danny sang in his chair, she pushed him through the park to the little duck-pond at the far end. She took him right up to the railings so he could chuck bread bits for the mallards there. It was April.

Daffodils blazed brilliant; pussy-willow hung yellow-flecked fur tails; everything seemed to reflect the sun's brilliance. It was not a day for sorrowing. Danny shrieked with excitement as sparrows darted round the wheels of his chair, pecking up the crumbs that he dropped. His bag of bread-bits slid from his knee, and he strained to pick it up. She watched, unable to help him, as he leaned forward and splayed out his fingers. Any further and the chair must tip. Still she didn't move. He tried to slide his body forward, using his arms like levers, pushing his feet towards the bag. Now the chair would tip. A little girl ran past, picked up the bag, and shyly held it out for him.

'I nearly got it,' Danny said. 'Didn't I?'

The child shook her head at him, wondering.

'It's not for me, anyway,' Danny said. 'It's for the ducks. D'you want some?'

She shook her head again, scared of him, but studied him as he threw the crusts on to the water and the mallards bobbed for them. Josie, on her bench, watched the little girl skipping, saw the tiny bulge of muscle on the perfect legs, and, for the first time, was jealous. The child toed her sandals on to the railings, hoisted herself up, jumped down lightly to scoop up the crusts that Danny dropped and to tease the sparrows with them, and then, like a bird herself, flung away from the railings up to the grass slope. 'I'm going to play,' she shouted. Danny bent forwards, as if he was too intent on watching the mallards to notice.

Mike came without Josie seeing him. He put a hand on her shoulder, squatting down on his heels next to her bench. 'What's Danny doing?'

'They've given him a wheelchair.' She couldn't find her voice.

'He doesn't need one. Not yet,' Mike said, angry.

'He keeps falling over. They said he needs one now.'

'Not all the time?'

'No. Not yet. But he's got to get used to it.'

She stood up and took Mike's hand, pulling him up and away from the pool so that they were out of Danny's earshot. Her fingers were tight on his wrist.

'What's up?' he asked, scared. 'What did they tell you?'

'Nothing we don't know. The same story.' She could still hardly trust her voice. 'Mike. I think I want Danny to go into a Home.' The child bending forward in his chair blurred. Points of sunlight on the water splintered and danced apart. 'I think it would be the best thing for him. Children like him ... his own friends.'

'You're tired,' Mike said.

'Yes. I'm tired. I don't know how long I can go on. I'm scared. It's too much responsibility.'

In the tree above them a blackbird's song broke out, brazen with optimism. Mike could only watch her, helpless, while she struggled to say what she had to say.

'I feel guilty for saying that,' she said. 'And I feel guilty for giving birth to him. Sometimes I think it would have been better ... if he'd never been born.'

That was the terrible thing that my mother said about Danny, and she said it because she loved him.

Relentless, the blackbird started his song again. 'He's my boy too, remember,' said Mike. 'We'll manage.'

'Daddy! Dad! Look at my chair!' Danny shouted. 'It's brilliant!'

That night Mike brought all the family together for a meeting. Josie cooked for them while he collected first Albert and Dorothy, and then Jack and Bridie. Danny was asleep in his new bedroom downstairs by then. Mike didn't mention what had happened in the park.

'We want your advice about Danny,' he said. 'He's only got about ten more years with us. We know that and we've got to accept that.' Albert watched his son, thinking how much of a man these responsibilities had made him.

'It's not long,' said Josie. 'What can we do for him to

make those ten years worth having?' Her young face was already lined with care.

'Seventeen years of life that's full and loving is every bit as good as seventy years of life that's cold and wasted,' said Bridie. 'He's a very happy child, thank God.'

Dorothy thought of old Mrs Beatty, who'd spent the last few weeks of her long life regretting that she'd done nothing with the rest of it. 'If I'd had a bit of cash,' she'd said, steaming her feet by their fire at home, 'I'd be off, here, there, everywhere. I'd be doing all sorts.' And Dorothy and Louie and the little ones had laughed, knowing that Mrs Beatty had never so much as wandered into the next street to see what was going on there. 'I was a girl then,' Dorothy thought. 'What's life done with me?' Silence droned in the room. They would give him everything money could buy. Was that enough? 'There's nothing more worth having than a mother's love,' Jack said softly. 'And a father's,' said Mike.

Danny cried in the next room and Josie went in to him. He had cramp in his legs from lying awkwardly. Josie massaged them for him, as she did every night. Usually they told each other stories, but not that night. He sensed her unhappiness and stayed quiet. His teddy-bear had cramp too, he said. He'd do what he could for him.

'Better, love?' Josie asked.

'Yes, thank you. Ted's better too.'

'Good boy. Try to get back to sleep now.'

Danny pushed himself on to his side, ready for the short sleep that would take him to his next spasms. Josie sat by him, stroking his hand.

'Mummy? D'you know what I want more than anything else in the world?'

Her heart stopped. Had the boy heard?

'What, Danny?'

'A baby sister. Can I?'

It was a terrible decision for Mike and Josie, my Mum and Dad, to make. They were warned that they could have another boy like Danny. They knew that even perfectly healthy children would be a terrible strain on their energies. But all the grandparents would help. It was a family decision. A year later, then, John was born; a big baby, quiet and sullen and always independent. I was born ten months later. From the first moment I breathed, I was the best thing that had ever happened to Danny. 'Is she really mine?' he asked, as I was put into his arms to nurse. He gave me his teddy-bear, and he gave me my name: Jess. For most of my childhood we slept in the same bedroom.

My mother, up to her eyes in work, was happier than she'd ever been. It didn't make things harder for her to have two healthy children playing round and getting in her way; it helped. Danny was never on his own now.

On Danny's tenth birthday Mum bought him a camera. All the grandparents came to the party and afterwards, because it was a warm, rich September afternoon, we all went into the garden. The apple trees were heavy with red globes of fruit, like a Christmas tree hung with baubles. Dad picked some down for us all, but because I was three I wanted the big red one near the top.

'I'm not getting the ladders out,' Dad said. 'Have one of these or do without.'

I sat by Danny's chair and sulked, till he suddenly took Ted out of my arms and flung him up the tree, hoping to knock the apple down. He didn't, of course. Ted dangled, upside-down, and way above the tantalising apple. I punched his arm in anger, and suddenly Grandad Albert lifted me up and ran with me to the tree, holding me on his shoulders. I still couldn't reach.

'Throw her up, too, Grandad!' Danny shouted. I looked down from my great new height and saw everyone laughing up at me, and I started crying, which made them laugh even more. John ran to get one of the crutches that Danny sometimes used and danced round Grandad, waving it, and I grabbed it off him and swung it up high.

'Give it a good swipe! Whack it, Jess. You're rubbish!' Danny was giggling with excitement, rolling the chair backwards and forwards round Grandad's legs to stop us getting near enough to the tree. I hurled the crutch and it smashed against the tree, toppling down into next door's garden. The apple I'd been after dropped on to Grandad Albert's head and then smashed in a pulp on to the path, but Ted still swung like a hanged man by his braces, and I howled.

'It had maggots in it anyway,' said Grandad Albert. 'I've just found one in my hair.'

Danny held his arms up for me, shrieking with helpless laughter, and that was when my mum took his photograph.

As John grew older he hated to be in the house. He was always off somewhere, playing football or something, but I preferred to stay in with Danny. We were very alike. We used to paint together for hours, or he'd read to me. If we went to the park I'd push Teddy in my toy push-chair, which Dad had specially adapted with pram wheels to make it look like Danny's wheelchair. John would be running round playing, and I would sit on the park bench next to the two wheelchairs, chattering to Danny.

'Don't you want to go and play?' he'd say sometimes.

'Not if you don't,' I'd say.

He'd pretend to think about it. 'No. I don't feel like it today,' he'd say.

'Neither do I,' I'd say.

But I did feel like it. When Danny wasn't with me I'd race across the park like a bird set free. I'd call it 'running for Danny'.

In the year that I was eight Danny deteriorated rapidly. I always used to run home from school, straight in to talk to Danny. Now my prattle started to annoy him. He seemed to have no time for me. Mum would send me scurrying out

Danny of the room as soon as she saw him growing tired.
John would be out somewhere else, away, always away till
mealtimes. I used to sit on the outside window-ledge
watching my mother washing and changing Danny, who
was nearly seventeen; nearly a man. He had no strength in
his limbs. I used to wait for him to wave to me or call me
back in to play with him, but these days he never did. It
took him all his energy to be lifted and rolled by my mother
back into his chair, and there he would lie, limp and
drained, sleeping from time to time. My mother never left
him. She would wheel him into the kitchen and watch him
anxiously while she prepared his food, and then she would
kneel beside him, coaxing him with spoonfuls that she'd
mashed into a soupy pulp, like baby food. It would trickle
from his mouth and she would scoop it up on the side of the
spoon and not scold him. I would have been able to do that
for him, if she'd let me.

'Get your own,' she'd say to me when she realised I was
hovering near, watching. 'Don't hang round me, for
goodness' sake.'

As soon as my dad came home he would make Mum go
upstairs for a little sleep and he'd sit on the chair opposite
Danny, and lean right forward in it, talking and talking to
Danny. It was as if there was a web of some sort round
them. When my bedtime came I would go to my room,
unnoticed, and settle Teddy down for the night.

There was no talking to anyone these days. When I had
the chance I'd take my little stool and put it next to
Danny's chair. Sometimes I'd slide my book across to him
and he'd push it back to me.

'What's up with you, Danny?' I'd ask.

'Nothing. I'm just fed up, that's all.'

And then one evening when we were watching television
together Danny slumped in his chair; just keeled sideways
as if someone had let the air out of him. My father lifted
him out and laid him on the table and gave him the kiss of

life. Danny's hands began to move and he opened his eyes, scared. Dad held him on his knees as if he was a small child.

'Not yet, Danny,' he said. 'Not yet.'

After that a nurse came in to see him every day. My grandparents were always in the house. And then, one weekend, John was taken to stay with my Auntie Maureen.

'Am I going?' I asked, not understanding.

'Danny wants you here,' Grandma Bridie said. 'He loves his little Jess, you know.'

'Can I play with him now?'

'Pop in and see him. But be very quiet, won't you? Don't make a nuisance of yourself.'

They'd kept the curtains closed in his room because the sun was so strong. There was no noise there. I was frightened. Danny was lying in bed, and he didn't look like Danny. He stretched out his hand to touch me and I ran away. I hid behind the coats in the hall. My father tried to coax me out, and I shrank in further.

'I'll take her to Maureen's after tea,' my Granny Dorothy said, and I knew I was being punished.

'I don't want to go to Auntie Maureen's. I want to play with Danny,' I said from behind the coats.

'There's no playing with Danny.' I could only see her feet.

'Why not? What's the matter with him?'

'Don't ask me that.'

'I want my mother.'

'Leave her. She's busy with Danny.'

'I want her now.'

'I said no, Jess. She's upset.'

I buried my face in the coat that smelt of my mother's scent and refused to come out. After a bit people stopped asking me to. The house was full of quiet bustle, and people coming and going, and whispering. I could see the door to Danny's room opening and shutting, and I watched the legs as they passed me in and out of his room, backwards and forwards, backwards and forwards, and I never saw my mother's.

Hours later the nurse and the doctor came together. The house went so still that I thought everyone had left. Then there was a knock at the door, and someone said, 'The ambulance is here.'

There were lots of legs then in the hall, too many legs, bringing something out of Danny's room.

'I hate my brother,' I shouted.

Someone dragged me out from behind the coats and slapped my face.

When they told me that Danny had died I knew that it was my fault. Nobody would talk to me and I knew it was because they couldn't forgive me for what I had done. My mother wouldn't even come down from her room. On the day of the funeral I sat next to her and my father, and Auntie Maureen brought John into the church to sit next to me, and because he wouldn't look at me I knew they'd told him what I'd done. They took Danny's coffin out to be buried in the earth and I stood with my back to it and nobody looked at me. I felt a terrible aching in my neck and my throat and I held my head up so I could see the clouds racing like blown smoke across the sky, and it seemed that the rooks gathering in the high branches were blaming me with their loud cries and that the dark trees themselves were pushing down on me, to crush me with their blackness.

And when we went back to the house, I crept away from the people and went into Danny's room and sat there holding the silence in my open hands and on my eyelids and on my tongue, and nobody came to find me. It grew dark and I went up to my room and nursed the teddy-bear that Danny had given me. Someone opened my door and I pretended to be asleep and they didn't try to wake me up. When I opened my eyes I could see the moon spinning like a Catherine wheel in the black well of the sky.

When I woke again it was morning. John was sitting on my bed.

'I can't cry,' he said. 'Can you?'

I shook my head, scared again. 'I killed him,' I whispered.

He stared at me. 'No, you didn't.'

'I did. I said a terrible thing. I did it.'

Someone else was awake. The waterpipe shrieked as a tap was turned on. Dad, it would be, in the kitchen. John pulled my eiderdown up over his shoulders.

'Auntie Maureen said that everyone knew Danny was going to die. Even Danny,' he said.

'Are you sure she said that?'

'But we didn't know. That's not fair, is it? They should have let us say goodbye to him.'

I had been in his room. I pushed the thought of it away; my terror. I jumped out of bed and went to the window. It was full morning. The grass was bright with dew. Flowers hung limp after their rioting in the night's wind.

'Will you put your shoes on,' I said to John, 'and come out into the garden with me?'

Dad must have taken a drink up to Mum, because he wasn't in the kitchen when we went down. I was carrying Ted. We went out into the garden and found a spade and fork and chose a spot together. Then I put Ted down on the wet grass and we both dug, bringing up the brown, moist earth, each with our own thoughts busy in our heads. Mud spattered the hem of my nightgown. We turned up bulbs as we dug and I put them carefully to one side for replanting, glad that there would be flowers there.

'That'll do,' John said.

We put down the spade and fork and I picked Ted up.

'Goodbye, Danny.'

I laid Ted gently into the soil, tucking his torn leg down so he would be comfortable. We scooped up the rich earth and sprinkled it onto him.

'Ashes to ashes . . . .'

I had that terrible aching in my throat again, and then I heard John sob, and when at last the sweet relief of tears washed down my face I felt as if the crying would never end.

My mother came out to us in her nightdress and bare feet and her hair all loose and tousled. She drew us both in to her.

'Time for the living,' she said. 'I hope it's not too late.'

7 Bird Boy

In cruel contrast to Danny, my other brother John is very active, healthy and strong. His great passion is cycling. I use my bike because I can't be bothered to wait for the bus, but Sheffield is such a hilly place that I end up having to push the thing half the time. But John is always off somewhere on his bike, speeding off to Ladybower or around Strines. We never see him at weekends. Mum gave up worrying about him years ago. If we ever happened to be all going out in the car together for a run into Derbyshire, John would always chirp up with travel tales like, 'This is where Haggis fell off his bike,' or 'See that wall? We sat on there to eat our Mars Bars.'

I didn't seem to have much in common with John. None of us did. I don't think Dad ever had much time for him. After Danny died, Mum and I grew to be very close; I loved to be with her. I even enjoyed going into town with her, just noseying round the shops, but most of all I liked to go out into Derbyshire with her for walks on Sundays. I sometimes wonder now if I annoyed her, always wanting to be with her and to do what she did.

'I'm never going to get married,' I said to her one day. 'I'm going to stay with you and look after you in your old age.'

She laughed. 'I hope I'll always be able to look after myself,' she said. 'But if I can't, I want you to take me down to Land's End and put me in a little boat and push me out to sea.'

'Don't be daft, Mum. You'd be seasick,' I said, but I could hardly hide the great cold surge of grief that came over me when she said that.

I was about thirteen then. We were walking in one of Mum's favourite places, on the top of Stanage Edge, where huge rocks poise in chancy balance over the valley. Below us we could hear the chink of metal on stone as climbers edged their way up like spiders, and the echo of their voices. The moorland was dark still with winter colour. There were humps of sheep and boulders in the heather, and away over the Edge afternoon sun slanted across rich green farmland. Spring had reached the lower slopes. Somewhere out there John would be on his bike, eating Mars Bars and counting up his miles.

Danny would have been twenty-three by now, I thought suddenly. I wondered if it still hurt Mum to think about him the way it still hurt and frightened me. Where was he?

'Do you believe in Hell and Heaven, Mum?' I asked her. She laughed again.

'It's coming out here that does that to you. Measuring yourself against all this sky and all these rocks, and knowing how tiny you are.'

'But *do* you?' I felt suddenly as if I was clutching hold of her to stop myself from spinning like a dust atom into the elements. I was dizzy. We sat down for a few minutes in a cradle of boulders, out of the wind.

'When I was your age I believed in Heaven and Hell. Yes, I did. I was a Catholic, remember. I loved the idea of reward and punishment. It seemed right, somehow, and neat. But now I don't know what I believe.'

I did feel tiny out here. I wondered if I mattered at all. One little white flower bell was still nodding in a clump of dead heather, and I thought, when all the moors were covered in heather, when it was all out, purple and white and sea-blue, with bursts of yellow gorse amongst it all, did anyone even notice this little white bell? I pulled it up to show it to Mum.

'Who matters most,' I asked her. 'Me or this bit of heather?'

'You do.'

'Yes, but how do you know I do?'

'I suppose because the flower can give pleasure, but that's all. You can take pleasure too. I don't know, Jess. Don't ask me hard questions.'

'I shouldn't have pulled it up,' I said. 'It'll die now.'

We arrived back home just after John. We saw him park his bike by the back door, take something out of his saddle-bag and run upstairs in front of us with it. He went straight into the bathroom.

'Have a good ride, John?' Mum shouted.

'Great! Forty-three miles.' He shut the bathroom door behind him.

It was his turn to help to get the tea ready. I stayed in my room doing some revision. Mum was a history teacher, and I'd failed history in the last exams. She didn't seem to mind, but I did. I was never going to fail again. Dad called upstairs to ask me to get a clean table-cloth from the airing cupboard in the bathroom.

'I'll get it,' John said, bounding up the stairs, but I was already at the cupboard. I opened the door and something came at me in a fury, beating against my face. I screamed out and John pulled me to one side. Mum followed him in.

'What do you think you're *doing*?' she demanded.

John was holding a grey pigeon. It fluttered frantically in his hands, its eyes bright with terror. I was still shaking. I'll never forget the thrust and flap of those wings across my face. Mum started to pull soiled linen out of the airing cupboard.

'How on earth could a bird get in here?'

'I put it there,' John said.

'In the *airing* cupboard!'

'I'm sorry, Mum. Sorry. We found it on our ride. Haggis thought it was dead and I thought it wasn't, so I brought it home in my saddle-bag and put it in the airing cupboard to get warm.'

'You're an idiot,' shouted Mum, as upset as I was. 'An idiot. Look at the mess it's made in here. Get it out.'

John stood with his hands clasped round the pigeon, holding it up against his chest so it looked strangely like a beating heart.

'Get it out!' Mum shouted. 'I can't stand birds in the house.'

Dad, still floury from the pastry he'd been making with John, came in to see what was happening. 'Get rid of it, John.'

'What d'you mean, get rid of it?'

'Take it back where you got it from.'

'Nearly in Grindleford, Dad. It's miles from here.'

'Get it out.'

'I want my tea first.'

'Your tea can wait. Get rid of it.'

John's face looked pinched and white. I was the cause of the trouble with my screaming, and I could have helped him to get out of it. But I didn't. I was pleased that they sided with me against him, protecting me from my fright.

'That was a stupid trick to play on me,' I said.

'It wasn't a trick. I put it there because I thought it needed some warmth.'

'And you've proved your point.' Dad steered him out on to the landing. 'Now clear off with it.'

I smiled at John as he went past, smug with victory.

Dark came fast, and still John didn't come home. Mum got her marking out and pretended to be engrossed in it, but she sat tapping and tapping the table-top with her biro and glancing up at the window which only showed her herself and us, turned in on ourselves. I wondered if John would ever come home. I imagined him cycling on through the night down all the quiet lanes of Derbyshire.

'Mum, help me with my history,' I asked her. 'I've got an exam tomorrow.'

'Do it yourself,' she said.

I flicked bits of paper at the cat, tormenting him, till Dad, too, snapped at me.

At last we heard the whirr of wheels in the passage. Mum quickly drew the curtains and turned back to her school books. Dad went to switch the oven off.

'Hungry?'

John didn't answer. He came into the room and flopped into an armchair, sprawling out his arms and legs. He was exhausted. His face was streaked with dirt where he'd been rubbing his eyes.

'I've brought it back,' he said.

Dad came in from the kitchen and stood in the doorway, too angry to speak. John gently undid his jacket and brought out the bird that was nestling there. He cradled it in his hands and it watched us quietly. Paddy, the cat, arched his back and bushed his tail out at it. I stroked him while he hissed.

'Why?' asked Mum.

'I took it back where I found it. It's *miles*. I put it back by the trees in that Longshaw estate and it just kind of settled down with its wings spread out, and I walked away. But then I went back to see if it was all right and it was still there, just the same. So I picked it up and just kind of tossed it out to make it fly, and it dropped. I thought I'd killed it. It can't fly. So I've brought it home and I'm going to look after it.'

'It's not your responsibility,' I said.

'Of course it's my responsibility. I found it. You don't expect me to just leave it there, do you, when it can't look after itself!'

I caught the quick look that passed between Mum and Dad, and couldn't fathom it. Mum pushed her books away, weary.

'Give John his dinner, Mike. I think there's an empty carton in the car boot. I'll fetch it.'

The pigeon rustled about in the carton on the table while

John ate and Pad stalked round the room, sniffing the pigeonny air. John spoonfed the bird some breadcrumbs and milk. I peeped in the box but couldn't bring myself to touch it.

'We'll get pigeon-lung,' I said. 'Then you'll be sorry.'

Mum let him take the carton up to his room in case Pad decided to eat the bird, and I believe John stayed awake all night listening to its scrabblings. I was swotting history most of the night. Next morning John took the carton down to the bike shed, and I followed him.

'Are you going to keep this thing for ever?'

'If it lives. Yes.'

'It's very weak, isn't it?'

I bent down to look into the box. The pigeon scuffled away.

'Lift it out if you want to. Hold it.'

'Not likely. I hate the things.' It perked its head, watching me. I could see the throb of its throat, like a pulse.

'Course you don't. How can you hate birds?'

'I don't hate birds. I hate the idea of holding one. It makes me go all itchy.'

'That's only because you're scared of it. What's the point of being scared of it? It's a waste of time. Sit back.'

I sat back on my heels and John lifted the pigeon out so his hands cupped the wings down firmly. He held it out to me. I had to take it, because if I hadn't the wings would have lifted up against my face again, and I was terrified of that. So I held it, warm and pulsing against me, a light, fidgety, frightened thing, and I clucked my tongue to it to soothe its fears. When we were both calm John took it from me.

'There. You'll not be scared of it again now.'

We all left home at the same time. I sweated through my history test, and knew I'd failed it again. At break John's friend Haggis asked me where John had gone off to, and I

88

guessed he'd be back home, watching over the sick bird. And that was where my dad found him at lunchtime. John was sitting in the shed with his legs sticking out into the sunshine, the pigeon perched on his shoulder like a parrot. When he saw Dad coming he stood up, ready to hide. But Dad had worries of his own. He didn't even notice the pigeon.

'Where's your mother?'

'She's teaching today, isn't she?' said John surprised.

'Oh, yes, I forgot.' Dad went into the kitchen and came back out with two mugs of tea.

'We're on strike.' He balanced himself against the dustbin and handed John one of the mugs. 'I've just come from a meeting.'

'Why, Dad?'

Dad gulped his tea down and swished the dregs over the dandelions. 'They're laying three hundred men off at work. And I'm one of them. That's why.'

'Sacking you?'

'Aye. You could call it that. They call it redundancy.' He pulled a head off one of the dandelions so it popped on its hollow stalk, and plucked the yellow petals away, staining his fingers as he rubbed them in. 'It's starting all over, John. Steelworks all over, closing down, losing men. God knows where it will stop. The writing's on the wall for us, that's what they're saying down at the meeting. Sheffield steel is going to be a thing of the past. Who'd have thought it? It's a bloody shame. It's a crime.'

John stared at Dad. It seemed he was more upset about the industry than he was about his own job. John didn't know what to say to him. The Bradleys had always been steelworkers. He couldn't imagine any other job for himself.

'Will the strike do any good?'

'No.' The dandelion head was a moist, tiny ball in his fingers. He flicked it away. 'But it's all we can do to show

how much it matters.'

'Grandad will be upset, when he hears.'

'He was at the meeting. He's upset, yes. There's a lot of people upset. There's going to be a lot more. We can't just sit and watch it winding down and down. I never thought it would happen.'

'I never thought you'd lose your job, Dad.'

'Let's have a look at that bird,' Dad said at last. He lifted it away from John's shoulder. John had brought home a bag of corn for it, and Dad cupped a handful on to his lap.

'You want to get her some grit to go with that,' he said. 'Pigeons don't have teeth.'

'Sorry.'

'I'm just telling you, that's all. You want her to live, don't you?' He spread out the bird's wings and examined them. 'She's lost some wing feathers. I thought as much. Looks as if some fool's clipped them on one side. That's why she's not flying.'

'Will they grow again?'

'Should do. But you're lumbered with her till they do. What good's a bird that can't fly?'

'I don't mind looking after her. I like her.'

'That's OK, then. You keep her. You don't mind handling her?'

'Course not.'

Dad smoothed the bird's feathers down into place. She was quite calm. 'I always wanted a bird myself. Not a budgie. Not that kind of bird. I found a sparrow once, when I was a kid. About ten. It flew into the side of a tram I was on and knocked itself out, actually – splat, it went, against the window. I thought it was coming right through! Anyway, I dashed off the tram next stop and ran back and picked it up out of the gutter and put it in my pocket.'

'Did you keep it?'

'I thought I would. I thought I'd have it for a little pet.

When I got home I took it out of my pocket and the blessed thing flew away as fit as a flea and I never saw it again.'

'Why were you so mad with me, then, yesterday, when I brought Grindle home?'

'Grindle?' Dad smiled. 'I suppose it was because of the way Jess was carrying on. But you're quite right. It wasn't fair.'

But it wasn't that, and Dad knew it, and John knew it too. If I'd brought it home they'd have let me keep it. Mum would have let me.

Dad put the pigeon down on to the grass and tossed the corn down from his lap. A few finches dropped down to share it, then lifted themselves away as Dad stood up again to go back into the kitchen.

'Pity to see that,' he said. 'A bird that can't fly. Bit like me, eh, now? A skilled man with no work for him.'

Dad went in to wash out the mugs. John sat on the shed step, knowing he should go back to school. Paddy lay, lazy, keeping an eye on Grindle. The bird hopped on to the step and into the kitchen and Paddy just dabbed a paw at it as it went past him.

'Even the cat thinks it's not worth bothering with,' Dad called. He watched John through the window; a thin, quiet, moody boy. Not a bit affectionate. Not like the other boy had been. He'd never really got to know this son.

'Hey. Shouldn't you be at school?'

'Yes, Dad. I'm just going.'

'Hang on, John. I've been thinking.' Dad came out of the kitchen, wiping his hands on a tea-towel. 'Before you go. It looks like I'm going to be having some redundancy money to spend. Want to help me?'

John was cautious. 'How d'you mean, Dad?'

'How about you and me getting some pigeons and training them?'

'Us?'

'Yes. Just us two.'

'Mum,' I said at teatime that night. 'I think I've failed my history again.'

'Have you, love? Don't worry. Perhaps it's just not your subject.'

'But I want it to be!'

'Why?'

'Don't you? Don't you want me to be good at it?'

'No, Jess.'

I didn't understand.

'Look, love,' she said. 'Just because I'm good at something doesn't mean that you have to be as well. I'd rather you were good at something I knew nothing about, something I was rubbish at myself. Like art. Or French. Anything but history.'

It felt like rejection, and it was, in a way. It took me a long time to understand. I was hurt when she started suggesting that I should go to town with Katie sometimes, instead of with her. She needed time to herself, she said, and I needed time with my friends. And while this was happening I watched John and my dad growing closer and closer, in a way they'd never been before. It was like a kind of dance; Dad was drawing John in to him, and Mum was slowly turning herself away from me. It was something deliberate that they did for us, and that we didn't understand. I watched moodily as John and Dad worked together on building the pigeon loft. They came in to meals with the smell of sawdust and cold air about them, and the joking that they'd shared out in the yard.

I went out into the yard one evening. The loft was finished and they were resting in the house, watching television. Dad's tools were in a corner of the loft, ready to be cleared up later. I hunted among them and a bag of nails spilled out its contents, so they rolled and clinked against each other on the floorboards. I picked one of them up, and a hammer, and scrambled out into the yard. I wasn't quite sure what I was going to do. It was a good night; the sky had the bloom of polished eggs about it, the way it had been when Mum and I had been up on Stanage together, the last time we went walking. The kind of sky that makes you feel tiny; a mote of dust on the earth. I knocked the nail into one of the posts of the loft; a chink like tapped china, with its tiny echo round the garden walls; then drove it in hard, so it rang.

When I'm gone, that nail will still be there, I thought. Earthing me.

Dad put his head through the kitchen window. 'What are you doing, Jess?'

I felt elated.

'Just finishing off your pigeon loft for you, Dad.'

Mum asked me to go walking with her again the day Dad and John went to fetch their first pigeons. We watched the hang-gliders taking off from Burbage Edge like huge and silent technicolour birds, casting swooping shadows. It was the end of the lambing season in Derbyshire; last time we'd come here there'd been a notice saying 'No flying of any sort is permitted over this slope till after the lambing season.' Sheep ran in fright sometimes, when the black bird-shadow hovered over them.

'I wouldn't mind having a go at that,' Mum said. 'It must be peaceful up there; just drifting.'

But the very thought of it terrified me.

The pigeons had arrived when we got back home. They were lovely; pencil-grey and pinkish white, and buff, and blue-green; and they were never still, with their fidgeting heads and the lift of their feet and their pertness; and the busy and comfortable sound they made. They'd never been out before. They had to know that our place was their home.

At the end of term John brought one of them in to school to give a talk about it at assembly; we were having a pets week. When he'd finished the talk he did something I didn't expect him to do – he walked over to one of the open windows and leaned out of it and threw the bird up, sending it home for the very first time. Then he raced off home after it, even though he knew that Dad would be there to watch it in; and, more than anything else in the world, I wanted to be there too, with them.

The pigeons became a bit of an obsession with John and Dad; they were always off somewhere, tossing them up to send them home; and we'd be there, Mum and I, watching out for them fluttering down.

Grindle used to watch out for them, too. She could fly now. She'd take off to the park or to the high trees nearby; she could have flown off for good, but for some reason she didn't want to. Maybe she thought of our house as home because we fed her. But I think she knew that John and Dad had bought their pigeons because of her; I think she felt responsible for them. So she timed them, just as we did, and when they were due back in she seemed to know, and she'd fly up and turn and turn in the sky and then swoop down to be first in. When the others come down she'd fuss and cluck round them, like any parent, anxious and glad to see her family safely home again.

8 A Lad of Seventeen

My Grandad and Granny, Dorothy and Albert Bradley,
live in a short row of terraces near Darnall Road. I love it
there. I often go over on my bike to see them. They've only
got a tiny garden, just about the size of our kitchen, but it's
a real little sun-trap. They like to sit out there on
deckchairs on sunny days when they've a few moments to
spare, and talk about family matters. Everything interests
them, like how my Grandpa Jack is coping on his own now,
and what our John was getting for his eighteenth birthday,
and how my friends are doing. It puzzles me, sometimes,
that they could spend so much time thinking and worrying
and talking about other people, but I suppose it's because
there isn't very much happening in their own lives to keep
them going. My granny doesn't get out much at all now,
unless she's taken, because her breathing's so bad. She's
just about had it when she's done her bit of tidying-up
round the house, so she loves to sit out and enjoy
Grandad's rainbow of sweet-peas, and watch the sparrows
and starlings on the wall. Grandad does all the shopping.

What he likes to do most is to walk into town along the
canal tow-path, and I love to go along with him. At the
Sheffield end of the canal the water's as yellow as
dandelions; I suppose that's with all the rust and
chemicals. All the reeds are crusted with yellow and where
they've been cast up on to the bank they look like long
strands of rusty wire. Grandad says if I fell in the canal
there I'd come out galvanised, and I believe him. There's
an odd smell, too, like ammonia and pig-farms. Nearly all
the works along the canal-side are closed down; industrial

monuments, my grandad calls them, great corrugated iron shells with pigeons fluttering in and out of tiny high windows. It's a lovely place, for all that. There's a big white mill with dozens of tiny dark windows right at the end of the canal, and when the sky's right and the water's still enough to reflect it, it looks like pictures I've seen of Venice. Sometimes you get sunlight slanting under bridges so the water beneath it glows amber. And if you walk the other way, towards Tinsley, it starts to open out like the countryside. You get ducks and geese on the water and bullrushes and teazles growing, and no end of butterflies dancing round the odd useless machinery of winches and sluices and all the clutter of the closed mills, and sorrel bright as sunshine sprouting in the brick-cracks. And always in the background there's the roar of the city.

Our conversation on these walks would nearly always follow the same lines. Grandad would begin by remembering his early days there, when all the mills would be working and there'd be the throb of machines and a constant clanging and clattering along the wharves, and barges would be busy on the water. And then he'd say, casually, 'Are you courting yet, Jess?'

'No, Grandad. Not yet.'

'It's high time you were, then. What are you? Fifteen?'

'Nearly seventeen, Grandad.'

'Seventeen, eh, and not in love.'

'I don't know what love is, really.'

'You will. But I'll tell you one thing, Jess. It doesn't have much to do with kissing and cuddling. But I wouldn't expect a youngster of seventeen to understand that.'

No. I didn't understand him. Not then.

Sometimes on our walks we'd be joined by an old friend of my grandad's, an awkward, shambling, desperate sort of man, not a bit like Grandad. His name was Davey, and I wished he would leave us alone. He was a tedious talker, and I didn't like his white, mournful face. I always felt I had to talk down to him, as if he was a bit simple, though Grandad assured me that he was all there and not a bad lad. I couldn't see it. He spoiled my walks. At one time he had worked in one of those canal-backed mills. We would stop sometimes to have a rest on our favourite bench on the towpath and to share the doughnut that Grandad always bought to eat on his way back home. Davey would look at me sideways and swing his stick over towards the little red door of the mill on the opposite side. 'Are you watching, are you watching?' he'd say, and he'd swing his stick up and up till it was pointing to a tiny black window at the very top. 'That's where I used to stand,' he'd say. 'Right up there, squinting out at sunlight, till gaffer docked me money for wasting firm's time.'

I fancied I could see him there, white face staring, blank spectacles flashing back the sun, time-trapped in his seventeenth year.

'Bet you were dreaming about lasses, an' all,' Grandad would say, offering him his doughnut. Davey would turn his sheepish sideways grin at him, and then at me, only I wouldn't show I'd seen it.

'Lasses? What did lasses want wi' me? I've never got on with lasses, Albert.'

'Nay. But it doesn't stop thee dreamin' on'em.'

And the two men would sigh, and move their bits of doughnut round their teeth, and stare up at the little window.

I didn't like Davey, but I did like his dog. It's one of the daft sort that walks all over you. When we sit down for our snap it eats anything in sight; grass, paper bags, plastic pop bottles, anything. It ate my chewing-gum once, when I'd parked it on my knee for safe keeping till I finished my doughnut. He was welcome any time, but that lunatic melancholy of Davey's made my skin creep.

One day Grandad and I were about half a mile along the towpath on the way to Sheffield when Grandad said, 'Blow it. I've forgotten your granny's library book. Will you run back for it, Jess? Your legs are younger than mine.'

I don't run these days, I walk, when I remember to. He sat down on a bench to wait for me, and I set off pretty fast for the book. I'd just rounded the bend on the path when I heard familiar barking and caught sight of old Davey walking towards me, with his daft dog leaping round him hopelessly after butterflies.. There was no way I could avoid him, short of leaping into all that liquid rust. He saw me too, and mocked. As I approached him he straddled the path with his arms and legs opened wide in imitation of a gate.

'Got you now!' he chuckled.

'My grandad's on the bench,' I said.

'It's not your grandad I'm after. It's little blue-eyes!' he teased.

I stayed put, in half a mind to run back, and feeling silly.

'Come on, don't be shy. Give us a kiss for Christmas.'

'It's not Christmas, it's May. Let me get past.' I only knew him as Davey, but the familiarity of that name seemed foreign now.

He kissed his hand to me, in mock cavalier fashion, and suddenly my anger was up. I hated him, his old and ugly face with its white frost of stubble. Spittle oozed between the cracks of his yellowed teeth. His spectacles slipped forward so his eyes snapped shut and slit open again, wet and unfocussing. He grasped his stick between both hands and brought it up between his legs. I turned to run back to my grandad but the dog leapt up, traitor, and planted a paw on each of my shoulders, panting hot steam down my ears, frightening me for the first time ever.

'Animal!' I shouted. 'Stinking filthy animal!'

I pushed past Davey, sending him sprawling against the grass verge of the path, wishing I had the courage to push him in the other direction into the canal.

'Temper, temper,' he laughed. 'Can't a feller have a bit of fun?'

'Get lost!' I shouted. 'No wonder all the girls hated you.'

I ran off up to my granny's with the crazy dog panting after me and licking my legs, and Davey hooting his strange lunatic desperate laugh till far up beyond the next bend. I could hear the canal geese hooting in reply, sending the sound up like a siren of mockery and fear for me to hold in my head for ever.

My granny was asleep in her deck-chair. I found her book and hurried back along the road, the long way round, and came down the steps that brought me further down the towpath. I went back in dread to the place where I'd left my grandad. He was sitting on his bench still, dozing off, and there was no sign of Davey or his dog.

I had no way of telling Grandad what had happened. It sounded silly. He would laugh perhaps, and tell me that Davey wasn't a bad lad. I left it.

On our way back we sat down on our usual bench and Grandad got his bag of doughnuts out. It was a lovely afternoon, and the buzz of bees finding their way to the canal-bank flowers was soothing. We shared a doughnut, and then I waited, as I always did, while he sucked his fingers clean and read the first few pages of the new library book he'd chosen for Granny.

You sometimes get canoeists on the canal, and that was what I thought I could hear at first as a sound of splashing broke me from my daydream, but then I saw the yellow head of Davey's dog bobbing in the water. He paddled over to us and heaved himself out. 'Watch out, Grandad!' We both jumped up as the dog shook himself dry.

'Where's old Davey, then?' Grandad asked it. There was no sign of the man in either direction. The dog rubbed its wet body against our legs and set up a dismal moaning.

'Funny,' said Grandad. 'I've never seen dog without Davey before. What's up, old boy, eh? Sit down a bit, Jess. We'll wait.'

I sat next to him with a sick horror in my stomach. I

didn't want to see Davey again, ever. Nor did I want to know why his dog was swimming in that yellow canal and whining dolefully at our feet.

We sat. Grandad read again. I kept my eyes cast down, listening out for the passing of the three o'clock train that usually starts us back off on our homeward walk again. But then in all the heat of that May-time sun I felt the sudden chill of knowing that someone was watching me. My eyes darted along the walls and sheds and roofs of the mills on the opposite bank, and then to the little red door right on the water's edge, and up and up the rows of tiny black windows, right to the very top floor. The white face pressed against the glass stared down at me just as it had done in my imaginings so many times before – Davey, trapped, a lad of seventeen.

I nudged my grandad and pointed. He whistled softly.

'He's off his chump,' he whispered. 'Poor old lad. I knew it would happen.'

'Shall we get the police, Grandad?'

'No. Why get the old lad into trouble? We'll fetch him down and get him home to bed.'

We walked back up towards the bridge that would take us over to the wharves, with the dog snuffling at our heels. Before we left the towpath I looked back. I could still see the white face in the high dark window, and I fancied I could see the blank spectacles flashing back the sunlight.

I would never have found that mill. Grandad threaded his way through yards and over walls and round huge baskets of coke and stacks of rusted steel till I'd completely lost my bearings. We came to a fire-escape and a sign saying 'Danger: Asbestos roof' and saw that the door at the top was swinging open. The dog padded after us. Grandad heaved his stiff legs up the steep iron steps. I was frightened in case he fell. When we pushed open the door there was a fluster of wings as pigeons clattered out. The floor was partly ripped away. We found an inner staircase, then another, then another, and we stumbled up them in the lofty darkness. When we came to the workshop on the top floor we had no trouble finding Davey, even in that deep gloom. We could hear him sobbing.

'Come on, old lad,' my Grandad Albert said.

Together we helped him out of the building and into the sunlight. None of us spoke. Davey and Grandad made their way slowly, arm-in-arm, back through the maze of yards and sheds and over the bridge to our side of the towpath. Then I took Granny's book and went on home to tell her that Grandad would be in late for his tea.

When he did come home there was still some sun in the back yard, and he had his meal out there while Granny watched a family quiz game on television. I brought his mug of tea out to him before I left, and we sat for a little bit listening to the starlings in the eaves and to the rapid high laughter of the television programme from inside the house, and Granny Dorothy shouting out the answers.

'Old Davey won't be going down the towpath again,' Grandad said. 'No point, is there, if it upsets him?'

I sat on the step and sipped my tea. I wasn't going to say anything about what had happened on the towpath. I wondered if Davey had said anything, then. It seemed that Grandad knew.

'He's a funny old lad, Davey,' he said. 'Always has been. You just have to know how to treat him.'

I picked at a frayed bit on my jeans, not looking at him.

'Remember that do young John had, for his eighteenth. We all went to it; and some of your pals, and some of John's?'

I nodded.

'And your Grandpa Jack came. It was the first time he'd been out since poor old Bridie died.'

'We didn't really expect him to come,' I said. 'But he really enjoyed himself. He danced with all the girls.'

'He's got more energy than I've got,' Grandad laughed. 'And I'm ten years younger than him, and twice his size. It did him good, that do at the Co-op. But did you see him when he came in?'

I frowned, trying to remember.

'I did,' Grandad Albert said. 'And he looked lost. Little and old and lost; and I thought, all the fun's gone out of that little chap, now Bridie's gone. But that young friend of yours – pretty girl with curly hair – what's her name?'

'Katie,' I said, surprised.

'Katie, that's right. She knows a thing or two, that girl. I watched her. She noticed your little Grandpa Jack coming in and sitting down on his own, and d'you know what she did? She went up to him and put her arms round him. Did you see her?'

I shook my head. 'Katie's like that. She's lovely.'

'She is,' Grandad said. 'Some people have got that natural loving in their nature. She just wanted to make up to him for being old and lonely. And she did.'

He stood up and folded up his chair. The sun was dipping fast. 'What d'you think your friend Katie would have made of old Davey. Eh?'

I didn't answer. Grandad took his chair and mug into the kitchen and I wheeled my bike out of the shed. What would Katie have made of Davey that afternoon, if she'd been down on the canal-bank with him instead of me? She wouldn't have run off shaking and half-crying as I'd done, I knew that. She might have laughed at him, I thought, and walked back to my Grandad's bench with him. She might even have tucked her arm into his and called him her young man.

I tapped on their window to wave goodbye and pushed my bike out on to the street. Then I drove my pedals down hard so I was free-wheeling downhill with fingers of wind in my hair, the way I loved it. I think I understood then what Grandad Albert meant when he'd said that love was more than kissing and cuddling. I think perhaps that Katie knew that already.

9 In Fear of the Giant

If you climb up from our house and stand up on the Bole Hills you feel as if you could touch the moors with one hand and the heart of the city with the other, you're that close to both. From our street at night you can see a line of lights going up the hill and reaching out over Stannington, and you know that's a limb of the city, but below those lights it's dark and quiet with the secrets of the Rivelin Valley, with its hood of trees and the gleam of its dams threading out towards Ladybower and the hills of Derbyshire.

When I was a little girl my dad used to take me down Rivelin and tell me about the trolls that lived under the bridges and made the stepping-stones for little people to cross the river by, and I was half-afraid of them. My mother used to take me down and show me the remains of the old water-mills that have all been pulled down now; Swallow Wheel and Plonk Wheel and Wolf Wheel, and we used to search out the great round grindstones that scattered the river bed. She told me about a huge man called Uncle Gilbert who had red hands like bacon hocks with black hairs on the back of them. He used to work in one of these mills, she said, and he had a voice like a bull, and I was even more scared at the thought of finding him down there.

'Will he be there today?' I would say, when she took John and me down there for paddles and picnics.

'Not today, Jess. All the mills were closed down years ago.'

'But who is Uncle Gilbert?'

'He's my Auntie Louie's husband. Your Granny Dorothy's sister.'

'Can we go and see her?'

'If you like.'

'But not Uncle Gilbert.'

'We'd have to see them both, love.'

'Well ... what's he really like?'

'Like a giant, Jess. He really is.'

I was about eight when my mother took me to see them. It was about two bus journeys away, and it was the longest expedition that I can ever remember taking as a child. Nothing of that part of Heeley is left now, and there was little enough then, but the dowdiness of those streets soon dulled my excitement in the visit. Few of the houses looked like homes any more. Windows were smashed in or boarded up like blind eyes. Messages were daubed on crumbling walls. Whole rooms were exposed, with their floorboards pulled away and their wallpaper peeling off and their fireplaces filled with rubble. They were ghost rooms, and their occupants had long since crumbled into dust.

Only the marvel of the hills rising behind those derelict homes restored me – and there is always that marvel in Sheffield, with the promise of other things over in the next valley. The slope of grass by the church looked rich enough, even though when we walked past it from the bus we saw how thin it was, and how scuffed the earth was under it.

Before we went into Auntie Louie's, I looked back up the slope to the blaze of green and I was glad that she could do that too, every day. Her house and the one next door to it were the only ones left of a row of brick terraces. The front part of both was a shop, somebody else's, boarded up against vandals and daubed with red obscenities. We had to go round to the yard at the back, and this was overgrown with tall dandelions and rose-bay willow-herb as high as my head. Just by the back door were three or four crates of empty bottles, and a dustbin long since overflowing.

I have never met before or since the smell that sprang to us when my mother pushed open the kitchen door. It was the smell of sour milk bottles and stale beer, old cigarette smoke, newspapers and cats, fried food and something far worse and sickly-sweet at that. I took in the cooker caked black with grease and the lino curled back at the edges of the uneven floor, the rack hung low with grey and melancholy washing; the cluttered table.

My mum's auntie, tiny and bosomy and as wheezy as my granny, hair in white frizzes and no side teeth, clucked up from her black chair in front of the summer-time fire and hugged us. I looked round anxiously from inside her embrace for a sight of the giant, because I was terrified of everything my mum had told me about him, his bull voice and his enormous hands, the height of him stooping through doorways; the mockery of him. We could hear him all right, coughing in his room, and as it had a frosted glass panel I could see him too, the dark shape of him hunched over his table.

'We'll have tea,' Auntie Louie promised, 'when Gilbert comes through.' And, 'Gilbert will come through when he's hungry,' the bull voice boomed from the dark room behind the glass.

My auntie tittered. We sat waiting, listening to the drip of the washing and to a scratching at the skirting-boards. 'That's the rats,' Auntie Louie giggled.

'Not rats. Next door's cats,' my mother murmured.

'No, rats,' Auntie Louie smiled at me. 'I've seen 'em.' We waited again, while in his back room Gilbert the giant coughed his gut-deep smoker's cough. 'I expect you want to play the piano, don't you?' Auntie Louie asked me.

I looked at my mother, who smiled in amusement, and I was lifted up on to the piano stool. Its soft blue pile rubbed into my bare legs. 'I don't know how to play,' I said.

'Doesn't matter,' Auntie Louie said. 'Neither do I. Neither does Gilbert for that matter (though he thinks he does).' This last bit she whispered into my ear, a secret for me to keep, while she unlocked the lid of the piano and raised it up, and out of it flooded the scent of polish and lemons and old warm dust.

And as my fingers prowled up and down the notes, and away from each other, and in both directions at once, and my confidence grew and absorbed me, I forgot to watch out for the giant lurching through the door, forgot to be frightened of him, and only remembered when his big cold hands pressed round my waist and lifted me up moon-high on to his shoulders.

'This girl's got wet knickers!' the bull voice roared and, released by my disgrace, I was lowered down to safety again.

'He's a handsome devil,' my mum said when we were waiting to catch the bus again, and I wondered if I'd made a mistake about the meaning of the word handsome.

Years later when I was listening in to table-talk at home between my mum and my granny Dorothy, I heard that Aunty Louie had been offered a new house, but that Uncle Gilbert had refused to move.

'It's a shame,' Mum said. 'Auntie Louie can't wait to get out of that place, and I don't blame her.'

'Why doesn't she just go then, and leave him there?' I suggested. Granny Dorothy was shocked. 'Our Louie, leave her Gilbert?' she said. 'She idolizes that man. Idolizes him.'

'She must see something in him that I don't see, then,' I said. 'What a waste of time, living in that house.'

'He puts up with a thing or two, don't you worry,' my granny said. 'She was always a messy so-and-so, our Louie.'

'It's worse than it used to be,' said Mum. 'There's a war on between them, because she hates the place, and he won't leave.'

'Ah, there's more to it than that.' Granny Dorothy cast a quick look at me, and I pretended I wasn't listening. 'All that man ever wanted was a baby, and would she give him one? No. Why not? Because ... she's scared of them ....'

Their conversation drifted on to other things, but I kept that piece of information in my head because it interested me, and because I wasn't quite sure what it meant.

Sometimes Auntie Louie would come over to our house for tea. I loved her to come because she was so noisy and cheerful, and because she always had a bar of Cadbury's for me in her bag. Uncle Gilbert never came with her.

'Gilbert won't come out,' she used to say. 'And I won't let him.'

'Why not, Auntie Louie?'

'Because the vandals would be in like a shot. They'd rip the place apart.'

She herself would scurry home after tea with her handbag wrapped inside several layers of plastic carrier bags, and the handles wound round and round her wrist, in case she was mugged down her end of town.

'Poor Auntie Louie,' Mum would say. 'It's not as if there's anything worth taking from that house. She's nothing to be frightened of, really.'

'Except Uncle Gilbert,' I said.

I didn't see my great-uncle Gilbert again till last summer. It was a bruisy, thundery sort of summer, when everything was restless and uneasy. One day Mum had a phone call from her Auntie Louie.

'Jess, it's my Uncle Gilbert,' Mum told me. 'He's had a stroke.'

The picture of him, dark and noisy and scowling, came back to me.

'We'll have to go down and see him,' Mum said. 'He's in the Hallamshire.'

'Have I got to go?'

'Poor little Auntie Louie,' Mum said. 'She'll be frightened out of her wits. Of course we'll have to go.'

I knew why Mum wanted me to go with her. It was because she was still scared of Uncle Gilbert too. The bustle of the small ward was reassuring, but then we saw that there were screens round his bed. That makes your heart stop, always. We crept through into his quiet tent. There was no time beyond the measure of his breathing, and no focal point except the high bed and its huge dumped occupant. He lay back like a big limp doll on his pillow. His face sagged to one side, his big arms and hands were still. He seemed to be at peace, except for his eyes, and they, livid in a lifeless face, blazed black anger at us.

Auntie Louie was perched on a red chair next to his bed, fidgeting with his fingers, and when she realised we were there she turned and beamed at us. 'He's pegging out, Josie,' she said. 'Poor old lad. He's had it.'

I kept my eyes on him from my safe distance.

'Dear old Gilbert. He's just like a baby now,' Auntie Louie whispered. I waited for him to roar at her.

'Isn't this a lovely hospital?' she went on. 'Clean as anything. He couldn't wish for a nicer finish.'

I stared at him. The sagging mouth tilted, but no words came.

'He's as peaceful as can be,' Auntie Louie chirped. 'And all the nurses love him. Don't they, Gilbert? And he loves them.'

The bedside vigil continued. The two women chattered. I stared, uncomfortable, at the man I had never spoken to in my life. He lay back, white and passive, as his life drained away from him; and his dark eyes focussed on nothing and raged.

The heat in that ward was stifling. Mum opened a window behind Gilbert's head and the slight breeze from that lightly fanned his hair. Auntie Louie smoothed it back gently from his face, and giggled.

'Bless him. Doesn't he look clean? Ill as he is they've washed him all over today, and he's never murmured. They all say what a lovely patient he is. Just imagine! My Gilbert!'

Her voice prattled on comfortably. My mother's bunch of flowers rose and fell on Uncle Gilbert's chest. The tea-trolley trundled past.

'They won't be bringing any to him, of course. He can't even close his mouth round a cup. When you think of all the stuff he's swilled down in his time. Poor Gilbert, there'll be no more of that for him. Booze. Will there, love? Eh?'

Couldn't she see that passion blazing?

'Pity about the tea though,' she sighed. 'I could just do with a cup. I'd have drunk it for him.'

'We could slip down to the canteen,' Mum suggested. 'I think you could do with a break, you know. It's a terrible strain, all this.'

Auntie Louie jumped up, delighted at the suggestion. 'It's a lovely canteen,' she said. 'Clean! Wait till you see it. We can get a nice teacake in there, too.'

And off they went, little Auntie Louie as proud as a new wife showing off her house. We were forgotten, Uncle Gilbert and I. I stood in my corner of his tent watching the steady rise and fall of the flowers and listening to the drone of traffic outside, and with a sudden swell of grief and fear and without even looking I knew that Gilbert had turned his furious eyes on to me.

I wanted to run away from them, and to quench their black and terrible fire, and most of all I wanted to know what it was like to be dying behind them. His gaze burned into me as I tiptoed and settled myself on to Auntie Louie's chair, and as I touched his big, cold and hairy hand with my own and allowed my eyes to creep up towards his face our gazes met and fastened. I could have run away from him then; but this time, I didn't. Cold as death myself, I said for the first time in my life: 'Hello, Uncle Gilbert.' And then began the strangest conversation.

When he was asleep, some thirty minutes later, I went down to the canteen to find Mum and Auntie Louie. I wanted to tell them what we'd decided, but Auntie Louie was absorbed in the 'Houses and Flats' section of *The Star*, and was ringing items excitedly.

'Look at this one, Josie! A flat in Roscoe Bank! Couldn't be better – I'd love to be near Rivelin Valley again, after all these years!'

'Uncle Gilbert doesn't want to go there,' I said.

For a moment Auntie Louie stared at me as if she'd forgotten who I was, or who he was, for that matter.

'Wants? He doesn't want anything now, poor soul.'

'He wants to go back home,' I announced, but she was already on her feet, rummaging in her handbag for coins.

'I'll just give them a ring, Josie. It'd be a pity to miss this one.' She scuttled off to the phone kiosk. I picked the curranty crumbs off her plate.

'Doesn't she *care*, Mum?' I burst out at last.

'I think it's her way of coping with it,' Mum shrugged. 'Some people are like that.'

'I thought she idolized him,' I said. 'I think he's the one who idolizes her.'

We could see Auntie Louie from there, talking excitedly into the phone receiver. It was as if it was all over already; as if the awful part was something that she was never going to have to face.

'I wonder if she *liked* being bullied by him, Mum?'

'I think she did,' Mum said. 'She certainly doesn't seem to know what to do with him now he can't shout her down.'

'Except pretend he isn't there.' The thunder that had been threatening all day cracked at last. The wash of rain coursed down the windows, distorting the walls and rooftops outside. 'Poor Uncle Gilbert. She can't wait to get him off her hands, now.'

'I thought you were scared of him, Jess.'

'Once upon a time I was. Not any more. He's not a giant at all. She is.'

I sat back listening to the rush of the rain and puzzling over the strange thing that adults call love and which seems to bring the most unlikely people together and keeps them there, too. Auntie Louie bustled back from the phone, ready to dash off straight away to look at the flat at Roscoe Bank, in spite of the storm outside. I had a promise to keep.

'Auntie Louie,' I said, while Mum went off to get her another cup of tea to keep her indoors, 'will you take Uncle Gilbert back home?'

'How can I take him home? He's past it, all that. Why go home again?'

'It's the only thing he wants.'

Tears of frustration sprang into her eyes. I could see that the flesh around her face was beginning to shake, as if she was starting to lose control of herself. Mum came back with her tea and put her hand on hers to calm her, but Auntie Louie was having none of that.

'He doesn't want! How can he want!' she wailed. 'He can't even talk! How on earth do you know what he wants?'

It wasn't easy to describe how Uncle Gilbert and I had sat together and talked; how, in fear of the giant as I was, and out of some freak empathy with him that I didn't know I had, I'd kept my warm hand over his cold one and hadn't turned my eyes away from the fury of his and how little by little as I'd talked to him I'd seen the bright glitter in them melt away. I'd talked about the old mills down Rivelin, and what it must have been like for him to lose his craft when the mills were closed, and to leave the river and the quiet trees and move up to that tiny, dirty house that was his home. I'd understood a little then of what had always been behind that brawling and bully manner of his, and what it was that had kept him hunched over his papers in his dim back room, listening to the scratching of the rats behind the skirting boards and to my Auntie Louie's doleful exploration of the piano keys and submitting himself to the squalor of their slum. It was some sort of love that had kept him there, and her. Some kind of need they had of each other. And now he was alone amongst strangers, and he was afraid.

'Would you like to be back in your own house, Uncle Gilbert?' I had said to him, and 'Yes' his warm and grateful eyes had said back to me.

'I'll tell them, then,' I'd said, and at last he knew that he'd made himself understood, and had slept.

'He won't let me go' Auntie Louie said then. 'That's what it is.'

'He will,' Mum promised. 'You'll see.'

He did go back, but it wasn't for long. During that grey summer Dad and John travelled about England sending their pigeons home, and I was out most of the time with Katie. And Auntie Louie made one last sacrifice in honour of that something that had kept her and Gilbert trapped in their wretched cage together for all those years. She put him on an old couch pulled up to the fire, and played the piano for him, and enjoyed remembering their old songs. And then, when it was all over, she left that terrible house for ever.

10 Disco

One night after the lower sixth exams Katie came round to help me to get ready for a disco. About a dozen of us from our year were going. We'd had a few discos at school, but I'd never been to one in town before. Mum didn't really like me to go down town at night. I'm not too confident about dancing in front of other people, though I knew I'd be all right as long as Katie was there. She's a great dancer. When I go round to her house she always takes me up to her attic bedroom and puts a cassette on really loud so we can dance together. She opens her roof window so the music blasts out and up. 'Let's give the birds a buzz,' she says. Sometimes her brother Steve comes up to do some of his crazy dancing for a laugh. He's picked his style up from some of the black kids at school – it's terrific. You'd think his limbs were made of eels.

I was spending more and more time at Katie's house that year. We talked for hours about all the personal things we wouldn't tell our mothers. I don't know why, I hold things back these days. I know it upsets Mum sometimes when I go all moody and quiet and she wants to know why. Looking back, there was nothing to hide from her really, until that disco. Even then she'd have helped me if I'd talked about it. But I just didn't have the words to tell her.

Anyway, Katie came round, already dressed, to help me to get ready. I bought my clothes for the disco the Saturday before with my baby-sitting money. Clothes are cheap in town if you know where to go – we know the bargain rails off by heart. I tried them on the night before. 'How do I look?' I asked, posing nervously in the kitchen.

'All right,' Mum said. 'It could do with being ironed, though.'

'Mother! It's supposed to look like that,' said John. 'It's great, Jess.'

Dad didn't seem to notice, but later that night, when I was back in my jeans and sweatshirt, he said, 'You're growing up, little sprat. We're proud of you.' I'll never forget that.

When Katie arrived on the Friday she looked about twenty-three. Her perfume was like another garment, a floaty, shimmery one at that. I remembered what my Grandad Albert had said about her. Yes. She does know a thing or two. I felt childish and gawky next to her.

As it happened, Grandad and Granny were at the house that night.

'I'm coming up to watch the fun!' Granny Dorothy called after us as Katie and I went up to my room, and she brought herself painfully upstairs and sat on the bed to watch while Katie pulled my hair about to try to get it into a style. My hair is a kind of red-brown, and thick, and usually it just hangs. Katie blow-waved it so it swept back from my face. It made my eyes bigger and my cheekbones higher; I couldn't believe the difference. Then she started on my make-up.

'I'm not keen on make-up,' I said. 'It makes me itchy.'

'I'm not putting much on you,' she said. 'Don't want you to look cheap.' She bent over me, smoothing and painting as though my face was a canvas. 'It's fun, make-up. It's a way of exploring yourself. Look at that . . . .' She stood back to let Granny Dorothy see. 'You've got the same colour eyes, you two. That's the first thing to highlight, that deep blue.'

'You can do me next, Granny Dorothy giggled. 'Albert would get a shock! Do him good.'

Katie made me put my own lipstick on.

'Look at the difference,' she said, pleased. 'Lips are just

hems on your face till you put the colour on. Flaps to hide your teeth.'

I pressed my lips together to make the lipstick smooth and it felt as if I was being kissed.

I was a woman now, in that mirror.

'How d'you feel?' asked Katie, watching me.

'Itchy,' I said, screwing my face up to stretch the skin again.

My mum looked in. She's the one who's always taught me not to wear make-up. She never uses it herself. 'You don't need it, not with your colouring,' she's always said. 'It's bad for your skin. It's a mask.' But she sat next to Granny on the bed and said. 'Isn't she lovely, Dorothy!' and I knew then that she'd worn make-up too, at my age, and that she wished she was going off to a dance in town. 'I'll lend you some perfume,' she said, 'My special bottle.' I couldn't catch Katie's eye. I was always pinching that French perfume anyway. I thought Mum didn't want it; she never seems to use it. But she came back and dabbed it on my throat and the back of my neck, and then on her own wrists. She held her wrists to her face and breathed in deep, and it was as if the scent of them had made her dizzy.

'Now let's look at you, Jess,' Granny said when I had my new shoes on, ready. 'Your first dance!' And her blue eyes sparkled with memories.

We were just about to leave the house when the phone rang. It was for Katie.

'It's my mum,' she said, white. 'She's cut herself on a milk bottle and Dad's taken her down to the casualty at the Hallamshire. I've got to go home and stay with the little ones till they get back.'

I couldn't say anything.

'What about your brother' Mum asked.

'Steve? he's already gone to the disco. I'll have to go back.'

I thought I was going to cry. I couldn't help it. 'I'll come with you.'

'You will not,' she said, determined. 'After all the time I've spent getting you ready. You're going to that disco, Jess.'

'Not on my own. I'll stay with you. I'd rather.'

'I'll sit with the children,' Granny Dorothy offered. 'You can run me round there, John.'

Katie was nearly tempted. 'I'd better do it,' she said at last. 'Our Liam won't let strangers sit for him – he'd just scream and scream. He's a right nuisance. I'll come on after, Jess. They won't be long.'

She opened the door quickly before I had a chance to say anything.

'Hang on, Katie, I'll run you back.' John found Dad's car keys and ran after her. 'Have a lovely time!' Katie shouted, and by the time I'd pulled myself together and put my coat on they were off. I followed the car uselessly up the hill, and there was my bus coming, and other girls from my class waving at me from the top deck, and I climbed on.

I wish I hadn't.

I loved the music at the disco. It was loud and strong; angry sort of music. I didn't have to talk to the other girls. I didn't want to. The flashing lights were the colours of boiled sweets; they stained the dancers' clothes and skin with sliding blues and reds and greens and oranges. Everyone was watching a boy in a white shirt and white trousers; a poser. He jumped on to the dance floor and only the ultra-violet light stayed on, so his clothes gleamed like strong sun on snow. No one else could dance while he was on the floor. 'He doesn't half fancy himself,' a girl next to me said, and I felt embarrassed for admiring his cavortings. The strong beat of the music was like another heart beating in different rhythm to my own; it made my blood surge round faster, and sent a new energy bubbling up in me. I was excited just to be standing watching, aware of myself inside my perfume.

I looked round for Steve so I could tell him about his mum. Maybe he'd go home soon and let Katie come instead. When a new dance started and the boy in white leapt back off the floor I saw Steve dancing with some other lads from school, all in a bunch, and I knew I couldn't go across to him. Not yet. I couldn't trust my first stilettoes to get me across to him without slipping. He and the other lads looked young here, in their suits. Their arms and their necks were thin. Their hair didn't seem right. The girls from our class just seemed to merge in with the other girls and women. They all looked of an age here, and sophisticated, as if they'd left school years ago. They danced in a group, facing each other, turning their heads to see who else was there; they kept their handbags by their feet, and their shoes too, sometimes.

'On your own?' The loud voice projected down my ear startled me.

'I'm with them,' I said realising then that I *was* on my own. The other girls had drifted off to do each others' hair again in the toilets. I wasn't in their group, really. They'd forgotten about me.

'You look a bit fed up.'

'I'm not. I'm enjoying it.'

'Can I get you a drink?'

I was grateful to him for that. I'd never been up to a bar to buy a drink. At least I knew what to ask for. I knew what Katie drank.

'Cider and blackcurrant, please.'

I watched him while he pushed his way to the bar. I rehearsed what I'd say to Katie. 'This fabulous blond bloke bought me a drink. No, not one of the lads. You should have seen him, Katie. He was about twenty-five.'

When he came back the strobe light was on. The dancers jerked in a kind of monochrome fantasy, and in slow motion. The boy in white was in the middle of it all, everywhere, dislocated.

'It can bring on an epileptic fit,' the blond man told me. 'They shouldn't let it go on for too long.'

'It makes me feel a bit funny,' I admitted.

'Does it?' He put my drink in my hand and, quite naturally, slid his arm across my shoulders, protecting me. I was trembling. I was glad he couldn't see my cheeks burn red.

'Katie,' I rehearsed later, quite a few cider and blackcurrants later, when we were dancing very close together to a slow, sad song, and he was singing the words of it very softly, just for me, so his lips touched the down of my ear; 'Katie. I think I'm in love with him.'

He held my hand, not releasing me, when I told him it was time for me to go. I caught Steve's eyes, smiling, wondering, and I realised I'd forgotten to tell him about Katie.

'Happy?' my partner asked me. I nodded, nuzzling my head against his shoulder. I didn't know what happiness was till now. I was weak with it.

His name was Terry. He took me home in his car. All the way back up to Walkley I was snuggled down in the car beside him listening to his tapes, and to him singing with them. Once or twice he glanced at me, sending that weak rush through me, but most of the time he kept his eyes on the road, and I watched him. Yellow street lights stroked gold on his face and arms. I didn't want South Road to end.

But when we came over the hump of our hill and I saw all those familiar lights strung up over the dark rise to Stannington, and our own row of houses, quiet behind closed curtains, and our house with the gate half-way open the way I'd left it when I'd run out after Katie all that time ago, and a light glowing to show that someone was waiting up for me, I knew there'd be no lingering goodbye in the car.

'I'll get out here,' I said. 'You'll never turn it lower down.'

He put his hand on my arm. 'When, and where?'

'After school?' I suggested. 'Monday?' *Monday!*

'I'll be there,' he said. He blew me a kiss, and that was all.

I walked away, not daring to look back, and I listened to him backing round and revving up the hill again, and when he'd gone I ran down to our house the way I used to do when I was a little girl and bursting with things to tell my mum. Only I didn't tell her.

'How did you get back, Jess?' she called from upstairs.

'Someone gave me a lift.' It felt like a lie, even though it was the truth. My face flamed.

'Did you have a good time?'

'It was all right,' I lied.

I ran up to the bathroom and watched the make-up coming off and for the second time that evening I wanted to cry, though I'd no idea why.

'Katie! It was fantastic!' I told her the next day. 'He's better looking than anyone I've ever seen in my life before.'

I spent most of that day and the next wandering round hoping I'd bump in to him, imagining I saw him at the end of every street. I couldn't remember the make of his car, or the colour of it, or even, properly, what he looked like, but I could see the gold light of the street lamps flashing across his face and hands, and I could hear his voice singing sad songs down my ear.

Once I thought I did see him, and like a fool I ran and hid in a telephone box. I rang Katie, shaking.

'I've seen him!'

'What did he say?'

'Nothing. I hid.'

Mum wanted to know where I'd been all afternoon. 'Walking,' I said, and again my face blazed a lie that didn't exist.

Monday was the longest day of my life. Why on earth had I arranged to see him after school, of all places? I'd never be able to walk across that yard to him. Everyone would see him, waiting for me. Perhaps that was what I wanted, after all.

Katie and I skipped Careers in the afternoon and went to the toilets to put some make-up on. I made a mess of my lipstick because my hand was shaking so much. She had to smear it off with spiky school toilet paper and start again. She sprayed my hair into its back-swept style for me. I felt ill. 'It's that spray,' I said. 'You've used too much.' Then I snapped at her for using it again on her own hair.

'You've no need to use it. You're not meeting anyone.'

I noticed how carefully she'd done her cheeks and lips. Next to her I looked like a twelve-year-old with face-paint on.

'I'll wash it off if you like,' she offered. 'I just thought you wouldn't feel so conspicuous if I had make-up on as well.'

She's like that. I believed her. I just wished she didn't make herself up so well.

When the bell went for end of school we walked out with all the others, keeping our heads down. Steve ran up to say something but Katie shook her head at him. He gave me an odd look and walked off.

'I don't want to go through with it,' I said to Katie.

'Course you do,' she said.

'I think I'll come home with you and Steve instead.'

There were eight cars parked outside the school, and I didn't recognise any of them.

'He isn't here,' I said, glad, and a cold dismay in my limbs, and then he beeped his car-horn at me and opened his door. 'He's there.' I felt quite calm. I gave Katie my school-bag to take home for me. Terry leaned out to say hello to me and I glanced back to see what Katie thought of him. She ran forward.

'Oh no,' I thought. 'You're not having him, mate.' And I got in and slammed the door.

We drove up to Bradfield and had a walk along Agden reservoir. We were the only people there. I couldn't believe that I was there with him, and that it was all so natural, and that the warm feelings rushing through me and my tight throat were things that I could ever be in control of again. I'd been told that that fierce vibrancy was known as chemistry. Test tubes and bunsen burners.

'What are you smiling at?' he asked me.

'Nothing,' I said. 'Just happy.'

'I want to take you round to the heronry,' he said. 'Look. There's a heron now.' We watched the huge grey bird come in with its slow, heavy wingbeats and its long neck tucked down. 'Kaark. Kaark.' Its grating, desolate cry echoed across the water. It stood where it landed as still as stone, as if it had been carved there.

'It looks lonely,' I said. I found Terry's hand and held it, warm, in mine.

'It is a kind of sad and lonely bird,' he said. 'I know a lovely song about a heron . . . .

> 'The heron flew East, the heron flew West,
> She bare her over the fair forest,
> Lully, lullay, lully, lullay,
> The falcon hath stolen my mate away . . . .'

'Lovely,' I said, meaning his voice, which was light and natural.

'It's a folk-song. And a carol. I'll teach it to you, sometime.'

I warmed again, thinking of the days and months ahead, stretching into winter, and the dark nights of Christmas carolling.

'Ever seen a falcon?' he asked me. I shook my head. 'I knew a man who kept one, once.'

I wanted to tell him about John's pigeons, but kept it back. Not wild enough, I thought, for him.

'Do you know what your name is? Jess? It's a beautiful

name for you.' Again I shook my head. He slipped my hand out of his and then held it round his wrist, closing up the thumb and first finger so it looped him, like a bracelet or a handcuff. 'That's a jess. They use it in falconry. It's a strap of leather or silk that they fasten round the falcon's leg.

If I were a falcon, then you would be my prey
And I would hover, never to lose sight of you.
But if you were to be the keeper of my heart
Then my jess you would be, love, and I would fly to you.'

'Is that a folk-song too?' I asked, shy.
'No. It's a poem. I've just made it up for you.'
We wandered away from the reservoir and into the woods behind, which were deep in bluebells. We lay down in them and the scent of them nearly drove me silly as he threaded them in my hair and said they matched my eyes. I found myself talking and laughing in a new way, self-conscious because he was watching me all the time, and feeling now, for the first time in my life, that I was special. I felt as if I'd always known him, as if he was part of me, and that he knew me better than anyone else did. He knew a different me. He knew the person I was becoming.

'What time do you have to go?' he said, when the sun had moved away from us.

I looked at my watch. 'Six o'clock! I don't believe it. I'm sorry, Terry. I'll have to go back now. Will you take me?'

He pulled me up. 'Don't worry,' he said. 'There's tomorrow, and the next tomorrow, and all the tomorrows we want.'

We didn't talk on the way back. I felt we didn't need to. I kept the bluebells in my hair till we were nearly at our hill and then I let him pick them out for me.

'Tomorrow,' we promised.

I went straight to Katie's. I would ring home from there

and tell Mum she'd asked me to stay for tea. Steve let me in, and I was bursting to tell him about Terry. He knew as much about me as Katie did; always had done.

'You've got something in your hair,' he said. 'A bit of cabbage or something.'

'It's a love token.' I don't know why, but I picked the leaf out and gave it to him.

I rushed up to Katie, full of it all. 'What d'you think of him?' I said.

'Not much.'

'You're just jealous, then.'

She was quiet, absorbed in putting on her nail-varnish. 'What's his name?'

'Terry,' I said. 'He said I'm his jess. He's a falcon, and I'm his jess. Don't you think that's a lovely thing to say?'

'Terry what?'

'I don't know, I didn't ask. We had more important things to talk about.'

'D'you know where he lives?'

'No I don't, Katie. And I wouldn't tell you if I did.'

I sat, irritated by her strange quiet. I'd want to know all about him if it was her boyfriend. Let her stew. I wouldn't tell her anything now, anyway. She screwed the lid back on the jar, holding her fingers out so the polish wouldn't run.

'I wouldn't go out with him if I were you Jess.'

Anger and dread. Sick, the way I'd felt when I thought I saw him on Sunday afternoon.

'I suppose you know him, or something,' I said.

'Yes, I do.' Her voice was as tight as mine was. 'His name's Terry Goodinson. He lives off Crookes Road.'

I felt as if everyone in her house was listening. Everyone in the street.

Then she said, 'I know him because I babysat for him about a month ago.'

My mum must have noticed my face, blotched with crying,

but she didn't say anything. She brought me a cup of tea quite late on, and sat with me in my darkened room for a bit, but she didn't ask me anything. She kissed me goodnight, and that's something she's not done for a few years now.

I couldn't speak to Katie at school next day. I blamed her. She kept away from me till half-way through the afternoon, and then she said, 'Come on, we're skipping English.'

I stared at her, not understanding.

'Well, you're not going to leave school at the usual time, are you? You're not going to *see* him again, Jess.'

I didn't know what I was going to do. I wanted to be left alone. She didn't even let me decide, but steered me down the corridor as if I was an old lady on an outing, just being taken anywhere. I didn't care whether we were caught or not. Outside school I stared up and down the road, looking for his car.

'I'd just like to explain to him,' I said.

'Jess, there's nothing *to* explain. He's married. He's got a lovely baby.'

She did the same thing the next day, but on the Thursday she had a rehearsal straight from school. I ignored her instructions. I stayed in school till last lesson, and from the window I saw his car, prowling up and down the road outside like a stalking cat. So he was smitten too, as hard as me, and he was hurt because I hadn't been there, and he still wanted to see me. I followed the others out into the yard with legs like lead. My feet dragged the earth along with them.

Mum. What would *you* have done?

Then someone ran up behind me and touched my arm.

'Hey, Jess, wait. I'll walk down with you.'

'Steve! Not now. I want to go on my own.'

I could see the blue car pulling across. He'd seen me.

'Listen, have you heard this one? What d'you call a girl with one leg?'

'*Steve* . . . .'

'Wrong. Jean. What do you call a girl who catches butterflies?'

The car was idling, just a few feet away.

'Annette. Come on, Jess, you're not trying. What d'you call a bloke in a nappy?'

I shook my head. The tears were starting to come. The car horn beeped.

'Leave me alone, please, Steve.'

'What d'you call a bloke in a nappy?'

'Terry.'

'You've heard it before. Terry towelling. Laugh, then. What d'you call a man with a car on his head?'

Terry's car started to pull away, and I let it.

'I don't know, Steve. What do you call a man with a car on his head?'

'Jack.'

Stupid joke. Made me laugh till I couldn't see for tears. Steve was walking so fast away from school that I had to run to keep up with him.

'What do you call — .'

'Please, Steve. Enough.'

' — a burglar with a dog after it?'

'I don't know.'

'Terry-fido. Hey, Jess. I wanted to ask you something at the disco the other night but I couldn't get a look-in.'

'Go on, then.' Still laughing, don't know what at.

'There's a breakdance festival at the Leadmill on Saturday. I wanted to know if you'd come with me.'

'With you? '

'And John and Katie.'

'John and Katie? Since when have they been going out?'

'Since Friday. The night of the disco. The night they didn't go to the disco.'

'I never knew.'

'You've been somewhere else, Jess.'

I'd been far away. He was hauling me back.

'So will you?'

'What?'

'*Jess*! Come out with me on Saturday ... ?'

What do you call a girl who's attached to a bird of prey?

'Yes.'

He left me at the top of our street, and I went back home for tea. Mum was the only one at home.

'You all right?' she asked.

'Fine. I'm going out with Steve on Saturday, Mum.' How easy it was to tell her that.

'That's lovely, Jess. I like Steve very much.'

'So do I.' I was looking out of the window into the garden. We've got bluebells round the apple trees. They were just coming out. I turned my back on them. 'I can't think of anyone I'd rather go out with.'

11 Going Away

They all turned out to see me off, the night after the celebration party. We crowded together on the platform at Midland Station as if the party was still going on, shouting and laughing and telling each other jokes. At the last minute John and Katie turned up, arms round each other, and with them, Steve.

'I can't tell you how glad I am that you came down,' I said, hugging him. 'I'm sorry about yesterday. I did it all wrong.'

'So did I,' he said.

'I'll see you at Christmas,' I said.

'No promises.'

'Right. No promises.'

That was when Mum hustled me on to the train, and thrust a little present into my hand.

'Off you go,' she said. 'We'll never get rid of you, at this rate.'

They slammed the door on me and the train set off. Steve ran along the platform, waving and shouting till we pulled away from him and gathered speed. Going away, going away, going away. That was what the train had always said to me when I was a child, off on an outing.

But I wasn't a child, and I never would be, never, never again. The snake had shed its skin.

I opened up the present Mum had given me. It was the photograph of Danny, laughing out at me from the past. Danny, celebrating life.